Another Way To Kill
A Steve Dane Thriller

Brian Drake

WOLFPACK
PUBLISHING
— EST 2013 —

WOLFPACK
PUBLISHING
— EST 2013 —

The characters and events portrayed in this book are
fictitious. Any similarity to real persons, living or dead,
is coincidental and not intended by the author.

Text copyright © 2021 (As Revised) Brian Drake

Published by Wolfpack Publishing
5130 S. Fort Apache Road, 215-380
Las Vegas, NV 89148

Paperback IBSN 978-1-64734-726-0
eBook ISBN 978-1-64734-725-3

Another Way To Kill

Chapter One

The light over the fuselage doorway turned from red to green, and Steve Dane jumped out of a perfectly good airplane.

His insulated jumpsuit blocked the harsh cold of the night, but he felt the icy blast on his neck and most of his face—the only parts of his skin exposed. His jaw and lips felt numb. It would take all the Chapstick in the world to make his lips feel normal again.

Goggles with built-in night-vision capability covered his eyes. The goggles gave the ground below a greenish hue. As he fell through space, he scanned for a dot somewhere in the forest below. Dane pulled the rip cord. The parachute billowed out of his pack and jolted him violently as it blossomed. His descent slowed. He grabbed the risers over his shoulders and continued looking for the dot.

His lady and partner in crime, Nina Talikova, was supposed to be down there with the landing beacon. They faced a tense situation in Bogotá. But his night-vision detected no trace of the beacon. The light should have been flashing on and off in two second intervals. Had she been captured or hurt? If something had happened to her—

He found it.

The dot appeared off to the right, in a small clearing, which meant Dane was drifting away from the landing zone. It was hard to tell with nothing but black around him. Dane pulled on the opposite riser and drifted in the direction of the beacon. He'd land perhaps twenty yards in front, but that was fine. Nina had made the rendezvous. Plenty of other obstacles remained.

Jumping into Bogotá, or anywhere in Colombia, wasn't his idea of a good time, and his time in the Marines did not include airborne activities of any kind. When he began his mercenary unit, however, he had to adapt with the needs of his clients. Some missions required airborne activity, so he'd had to learn. The prospect of learning some new tricks had seemed daunting at the time, but he learned to jump well.

This time, he was jumping for one of his friends who was in danger of not surviving the next night. Devlin Stone, a man who had saved Dane's life more than once and responded to his calls for help many times without argument, now needed *him*. It was time to return past favors, but it wasn't as if Dane had been keeping track. Dane and Stone had worked together for many years. Their bond was tight. If Stone called, Dane answered.

Stone ran a smuggling operation throughout Europe, but had somehow, recently, run afoul of a Colombian cartel. Word from Stone's crew was that he was now being held hostage. Dane did not understand why Stone had been captured. The question could be answered later, and in as much detail as Dane could collect. All he knew right now was that his friend needed help, and Dane couldn't turn away. He intended to show up, rescue Stone, and kill whoever was responsible for putting his friend at risk.

The drug thugs seemed to have the upper hand. They knew of Stone's associates, and of his friends—like Dane and Nina and fellow buccaneer Todd McConn. All three had taken individual paths to enter Colombia as a way to avoid detection. Stone's people had set up a safe house and provided equipment. Dane, Nina and McConn were going to break Stone free and get to the bottom of everything.

A gust of wind kicked Dane left, further away from the beacon. He corrected with a pull on the right riser, keeping the landing zone in sight. Nina was taking a huge risk. If Dane could see it, so could anybody else.

The ground rushed up at a frightening rate. He pulled on the risers to slow the descent in the last second and bent his knees on impact. The jolt of landing rattled his bones. The impact wasn't easy to get used to and too much of it meant knee and hip replacements. In the future. If he lived that long.

Dane stayed on his feet, quickly detaching the rig. Anybody who later discovered the parachute would find it clean of identifying marks.

Dane ran across the hard-packed ground to the Chevy SUV twenty yards ahead. The motor turned over with a quiet rumble and puff from the exhaust port. He jumped into the passenger seat and yanked off the goggles. His eyes took a moment to adjust to the sudden low light in the SUV, the glowing lights of the dash. He grinned at the woman behind the wheel.

Nina Talikova, dressed in black with her long hair tied in a ponytail, didn't return the smile. Her face was a stoic mask of Slavic impatience. "You're late."

"I stopped for Starbucks on the way down," he said.

"Bring me anything?"

"I brought my fabulous ass."

She huffed. "I've seen better."

She faced forward and pressed on the accelerator, driving without headlights. Dane chuckled quietly. The terrain looked treacherous without illumination. Shadows concealed both dips and bumps. The SUV took the jolts of both well.

"Patrols are all over the place," she said.

Nina inched the vehicle along.

"Army, police, or cartel?" Dane said.

"It doesn't make much difference."

She slammed the brakes. The SUV jerked.

The headlights of another vehicle loomed ahead.

Dane put on the night-vision goggles and looked around. The low light in the cabin didn't give the goggles much to amplify, but Dane didn't need a lot to get a peek at the surrounding terrain and a nearby hiding spot.

"To the left. There's a cave."

Nina spun the wheel. "I got two AKs in the back."

Dane removed the goggles again and reached onto the rear seat where the automatic rifles lay. He grabbed one. She hadn't gone cheap on the gear, either. The "AK" was a new production AK-12 Russian automatic rifle chambered for the flesh-shredding 5.45x39 cartridge.

Instead of the usual banana clip, Nina had attached a 100-round circular drum magazine. The ammo made the weapon heavier, but the extra rounds might be needed in a protracted battle. Dane worked the charging handle and chambered a round. She had oiled the action thoroughly. The cocking handle moved smooth as hot butter.

Chapter Two

Nina powered the Chevy up the incline. The dark mouth of the cave opened before them. The SUV barely fit and part of the back end stuck out. She put the front bumper against the back wall and shut off the motor. Darkness closed around the SUV.

This is a lousy place to die if it goes bad, Dane thought.

"Too narrow to open the doors," he said. He climbed over the front and back seats to the rear cargo area. Nina followed with the second AK-12.

Dane and Nina scooted to the back window. Dane cursed leaving the night-vision goggles up front.

"We're sitting ducks if they open up on us," Nina said.

"Try not to be so optimistic."

Despite his own minor misgivings, Dane had no intention of dying in Colombia. And since he had Nina to think about too, he'd fight even harder. He had no intention of *burying* her in Colombia.

He had no doubt she felt the same way. Their adventures had taken them around the world for several years; they were permanently coupled; needed each other more than they both realized.

The other vehicle finally rolled into view. A military Jeep with four soldiers aboard. The jeep slowed. The man in the passenger seat stood up, holding on to the windscreen, and scanned the area. He took out a flashlight and shined the beam around.

"Somebody saw the beacon," Dane said.

"They're gonna see your parachute."

The jeep rolled out of sight. Then they heard yelling, rapid bursts of Spanish, voices rising to alert others. They couldn't hear everything through the glass and steel of the Chevy, but neither needed a translator to know what was happening.

"Found it," Nina said.

Dane's throat felt dry as he touched the trigger.

"I didn't jump out of a plane," he said, "to die in a cave."

"I'm not getting caught dead in this outfit with no make-up," Nina said.

Sweat dripped down Dane's neck. The passing seconds felt like hours. When you live on the fringes of the law, even friendlies can be enemies, and Nina's remark about the army and police and cartel not being much different resonated in the wrong way. The level of corruption in Colombia was legendary.

He'd survived many fights before, with Nina and without, and he had no intention of losing this one. Any doubts about his survival melted away as he focused on taking every necessary step to win.

Finally, they heard the jeep's motor rumble to life. The vehicle drove by in the direction it had come, the puffy parachute jammed between soldiers in the back seat.

"They'll report the landing and come back with a search party," Nina said.

"Is there another road we can use? They may set up roadblocks."

"Yes, but we gotta move right *now*." Nina left the AK with Dane and climbed back behind the wheel.

The SUV fired to life again. Nina backed out and executed a half-turn to drive forward again. Dane remained in the back to watch for hostiles.

"Let's do what we do best, baby," he said.

"What's that?"

"Raise hell and get paid."

"I knew I kept you around for a reason."

"For my ass, remember?" he told her. "You probably get a good look in the rearview mirror."

"Honey, you have a heart as big as your ass."

Dane chuckled. He wasn't going to let her get away with that. "Comparing mine to yours?"

She cursed him in Russia. Dane laughed.

Nina steered through cobblestone city streets with Dane lying low in the back. The SUV rocked gently as it passed over the stones. The wide sidewalks could accommodate plenty of pedestrians, though at this hour of the morning all the normal people were still sleeping. Getting two motor vehicles to pass comfortably was asking too much, and Dane tensed around every turn. They didn't need anybody coming from the other direction to slow them down.

Nina turned up an incline, made the next right and kept climbing. The short buildings on either side were sandwiched together with virtually no gaps between them, save for narrow alleys here and there.

"Where are we going?" Dane said.

"Top of the hill," Nina said.

Ask a stupid question. . .

The safe house had been provided by Stone's people, who also had transportation out of the country standing by, waiting for Dane's call. When they had contacted Dane to enlist his help, they offered payment. Dane turned them down. He didn't want money. His friendship with Stone meant more than cash.

Of course, Nina hadn't liked that.

"He at least owes us a case of wine," she'd said. "A girl needs her vitamins."

"What do you mean, *us*?"

She dismissed him with a wave. She knew Dane too well to argue very long.

Nina finally pulled into an open carport beneath an upper-level apartment. The outside showed a lot of faded paint, with the steps leading to the front door landing rotting in spots. A short deck wound around the front door to a large living room window overlooking the street.

"Spared no expense," Dane said.

"It's nicer on the inside."

"You mean *bigger* on the inside."

"That's a different series."

Nina told him to cover the weapons in back with a blanket and carry the blanket upstairs. She used a key to get in.

"Honey, we're home!" she said.

No lights in the living room. A short hallway led to a lighted kitchen. The wooden cabinetry had been painted a gaudy white and the tiled floor had seen better days, but otherwise it looked fine. Dane set the blanket-wrapped AK-12s on the floor near the door.

Todd McConn lifted a whistling teakettle off the yellowed stovetop. "Just in time," he said, and poured three mugs. He wore a T-shirt, jeans and cowboy boots—his usual uniform. His normally close-cropped hair had grown a bit shaggy.

Dane stood by the wobbly kitchen table and stripped off the jumpsuit, revealing jeans and a black T-shirt underneath. He left the jumpsuit on the floor, gladly accepting the offered mug. English breakfast, a favorite blend, second to any green tea he could get.

Dane and McConn sat while Nina took a moment to get a bottle of vodka from a cabinet. She touched up her tea and returned the bottle. Dane watched her over the rim of his mug as he tasted the hot brew. She avoided his eyes.

"How is the neighborhood?" Dane said.

"Families, working class," Nina said. "Lots of kids kicking a ball around during the day."

"We're in a perfect spot," McConn said. "Got surveillance set up on the target. Cameras on the roof. Lots of notes and pictures."

"Any sign of Dev?"

"Not yet."

"Do we know why the cartel grabbed him?"

"I've been poking around," McConn said. "He's never touched drugs in the past, so it's strange this happened. A fellow named Ramon Coda runs the cartel. He's been buying up or taking over smuggling operations around the world. Got his hooks in Asia and most of Central America, but nothing in Europe."

"He wants Dev's business?" Dane said. "That would never happen."

Nina said, "Which cartel?"

"South Coast Cartel," McConn said. "Made up of leftovers from the Celi and Norte del Valle cartels, which no longer exist." McConn sipped his tea. "One thing we do know is that they're moving Dev in two days."

"Where?" Dane said.

"To a camp in the mountains. Their version of 'enhanced interrogation' takes place there."

"If we find ambush points along the route they'll take," Nina said, "hitting them on the way might be the best bet."

"But?" Dane said.

"We'll have cartel and army forces on us faster than you can blink if we aren't quick."

"I want to see the route tomorrow morning," Dane said.

"Okay," McConn said.

Dane finished his tea. "Bathroom?"

"Down the hall," Nina said.

Chapter Three

Dane joined McConn in one of the other bedrooms where McConn had the surveillance equipment set up, a row of monitors showing images from three hidden cameras, along with panels to control the angles.

The set-up reminded Dane of McConn's "home" office, what he called the Memphis Strongbase. McConn, like Stone, had once been part of Dane's mercenary unit, the 30-30 Battalion. When Dane disbanded the unit, Stone went one way, and McConn another. Whereas Stone smuggled contraband, McConn traded a currency of information and intelligence.

But he could fight, too, when required.

"Ramon Coda lives in this house on top of the mountain," McConn said. He opened a picture of the house on a laptop beside the monitors. "House sits at the top, forest on all sides."

Dane didn't see a road leading to the house. "How do you get in and out?"

"See this cable car? It goes up and down the hill with entry and exit points at the house and bottom of the hill—

which also serves as Coda's parking lot. He keeps four vehicles there, three SUVs for the troops and his own armored sedan."

The monitors didn't show much because of the dark, but McConn ran back footage from earlier in the day and Dane watched the comings and goings around the house. No sign of Devlin. Where did they have him?

Dane climbed into bed after a hot shower. Nina had opened the windows, but humidity still hung thickly in the air. Dane eased under the sheet next to the snoring Nina.

As he often thought, she sounded like a chainsaw stuck in a log when she snored. She awoke long enough to roll over and lie against him. She wore nothing under the sheet. The humidity made her sticky skin feel good against his, although the heat of her body quickly became too much for the night and he inched away from her.

Dane didn't have many friends, and the ones he did have he wanted to keep. Too many, over the years, had either gone bad or wound up dead. He didn't want to add Stone or McConn to the list of the latter. He probably didn't need to worry about Nina the Indestructible, even though he did. How many times could they charge into a pack of hungry lions and make it to the other side?

She snored into his neck.

Dane took a deep breath and tried to doze off.

Nina jolted away in the middle of the night and let out a short scream.

Dane sat up as she rolled away from him, taking most of the sheet with her. He touched her bare right arm. "You okay?" he said.

She curled up. "Just a nightmare." She shut her eyes. "Go back to sleep."

"Uh-huh." Dane lay down again. He didn't bother to reclaim any of the covers. He stared at the ceiling. She was always having nightmares. She never talked about them or what might be causing enough torment to bring them on.

It worried him a lot. It worried him more than losing her, because she was dealing with an enemy neither of them could see. How long before the ghosts overcame her ability to resist?

Kids in the street kicked a soccer ball back and forth to each other, the ball skidding or flying across the street at equal intervals. The kids scattered when McConn pulled out of the garage. They took over the street again once he had driven away.

Dane lit an H. Upmann and blew smoke out the window as McConn negotiated the narrow streets, pausing often for the crush of pedestrians who owned the roads.

"Rush hour here," McConn said. "Lots of walking."

McConn finally made it through town and onto the motorway, where he took a turnoff onto a two-lane road after thirty minutes.

"This is the route they'll take?" Dane said.

"It's the only route they *can* take," McConn said.

McConn followed the road as it inclined, thick forest dominating the terrain on either side.

"There's a downgrade coming up," McConn said, "and then a flat section before the road ends and you get a dirt path."

McConn slowed at the top of the incline, eased the Chevy over and shifted into second gear as they started down the other side. He tapped the brakes now and then.

Dane scanned both sides of the forest. On the plus side, there were no gaps or obvious spots within the thick vegetation where a gun crew might hide. Downside, it meant that any crew that tried to set up an ambush faced natural obstacles that might get in the way of clear shooting. And if they tried to clear a spot, open an area only a little, they wouldn't fool any sharp-eyed soldier for one second.

Nina had been right about the idea, but he had to reject the plan after seeing the environment first-hand.

"Lousy place to set up an ambush," Dane said.

McConn upshifted as the ground flattened out. It went straight ahead for at least two miles. He took the drive slowly to give Dane time to examine the roadside some more.

"Stop a second."

McConn braked.

"This spot might work," he said. "Mid-section of the road, after they clear the grade. What kind of gear do we have?"

"RPG-7 and assorted small arms."

Dane looked through the back window, then forward again. "Pull off and see if we can find a landing zone."

McConn parked on the shoulder but said, "Let's have technology do some of the work, you dinosaur. Just sit there and smoke." He turned on the Chevy's GPS and tapped a finger on the screen to bring up a map of their immediate area. It wasn't just a map but a detailed satellite picture.

With his finger dragging the screen, McConn cycled the image and zoomed on potential spots. None looked appropriate enough for a chopper landing until the fourth option, but it was nearly two miles from where they were parked.

Two miles north.

"How close will that landing spot put us to the camp they're taking Dev to?" Dane said.

"Very close. You can see worn paths here and there that look like they were made by vehicles."

"It's probably the cartel's landing zone."

"The three of us can't take the camp. We can get more of Stone's people here, but that will take time."

"I'm not suggesting we hit the camp. This is a good spot. What we need to do is save the RPGs for the escape, in case cartel troops come at us."

"Okay."

McConn made a U-turn and started back along the road.

"Plenty to go wrong," McConn said. "They'll use at least two of the SUVs, but which one will Dev be in?"

"Another question. Are those SUVs armored like the sedan? Will Dev be in any condition to help when the shooting starts? Will we hit Dev by accident?"

"Whoa, Steve—"

"A lot could happen, Todd. We have to find a way to minimize the risks. Maybe your surveillance could fill in some gaps."

Dane tugged on the right sleeve on his shirt. He used long sleeves to cover the burn scars that started on his right arm and went up to his neck. A reminder that he might have survived the worst, but he wasn't invincible. If they stormed the castle without proper planning and precautions, their mission in Colombia might be over in the blink of an eye.

Chapter Four

Devlin Stone had long since given up finding a comfortable way to wear chains.

They had placed him in an adobe shed near the edge of the estate, where cartel leader Ramon Coda kept his horses. If the chains were bad, the smell of three horses and the buzzing from the accompanying flies were far worse.

Some of those flies swirled around him as he stood secured to a wall, arms up crucifixion-style, with his legs spread apart like a V. If he slumped, pressure on his hips made that position unbearable. If he stayed upright, pressure on his back. He alternated and tried to make the best of it.

They let him down once a day to eat while two armed guards who looked like they knew their business kept watch at all times.

Those two guards approached through the archway of the shed, a third man holding a tray of food. Stone blinked. The man was Coda.

"Hello, Mr. Stone. How are you today?"

Coda was short and round with close-cropped hair, the

opposite of Stone's shaggy top.

One of the guards slung his rifle and unlocked the chains. Stone collapsed on the ground, gasping.

"We can end this unpleasantness," Coda said, "if only you give me what I want."

"No," Stone rasped.

"You know I'm having you moved tomorrow, to one of our camps from which nobody will ever see you return. After that, I *take* what I want."

"I have friends who will disagree with that."

"We're watching for your friends, those loyal people you speak so highly of. They are not here. They have abandoned you. You are all alone, Mr. Stone. Give me what I want. I offered a fair price. Now I will trade your life for your business. Deal?"

Stone brushed back his hair with a shaking hand. "No."

Coda sighed. He placed the tray on the ground. "That will be your last meal. Now I must make plans on how best to kill the rest of your people when I march into your headquarters and announce that *I* am the new boss."

The cartel leader marched out and the guards remained. Eventually Stone began to eat, but he could hardly lift the fork to his mouth. He made it happen, but slowly, and painfully. His whole body agonized with each movement.

Of course, he knew he hadn't been abandoned. Dane would show up alone, if nothing else. He only had to hold on a little longer. A rescue during transit was a sure bet—if Dane knew about it. That was the only catch.

Ramon Coda walked away from the shed lamenting that such unpleasantness was required.

He followed the dirt path through a garden and stopped at the edge where a low wall of brick had been built. It marked the edge of the property and the beginning of a steep drop off into oblivion. The blanket of green forest sprawling to infinity before him helped him sort his thoughts.

He needed a way out of Colombia. The US had stepped up its anti-drug efforts, augmenting Colombian forces with special operations units that were wiping out even Coda's trained fighters, and he'd hired the best European mercenaries money could buy to train his army.

Getting out of Colombia and surviving and thriving meant making connections in Europe. That meant getting rid of the competition one way or another; so far, he'd bought out or killed those who stood in his way. It appeared the Devlin Stone would soon count himself among the latter.

And it was a shame, because Coda hated to waste bullets in such trivial matters. He was offering good money for peoples' businesses. Some had realized the opportunity to get out of the business with their freedom intact.

Some were simply too stubborn.

He let out a sigh. The unpleasantness would end soon, and he'd take what he had so generously offered to purchase. Such was life.

Coda turned from the forest view and headed back for the main house.

Dane and McConn brought lunch back to the safe house and found Nina in front of McConn's monitors.

"What did you find?" she said.

Dane handed her a large burrito. McConn cleared space on the table. He sat there while Dane sat next to Nina in front of the TVs. They ate on their laps.

Dane brought her up to date.

"I saw something that will help," Nina said. She used a joystick to move a camera and then zoomed in to a shot that showed an adobe shed set away from the main house.

"Coda brought a tray of food in there," Nina said. "He left alone. The two guards left later with the empty tray."

"How many troops at the estate, Todd?"

"About twenty," McConn said.

Dane cursed. "And going up and down that mountain will be tough. The cable car is a death trap."

"They'll have to bring Dev down in that cable car to the parking lot," Nina said. "What is we take out the control cables and trap them on top?"

"That would work unless they have another way down that we don't know about," Dane said.

"Then we'll have to take our chances on the travel route," Nina said. "They have no options there."

"Setting up an ambush there isn't going to be easy."

"Then what's your idea? So far, all I've heard from you is what *won't* work."

Dane sighed. "You're right. Let me look over the options myself and see if anything comes to mind."

"We're running out of time, Steve."

"I know. Isn't this a good burrito?"

Nina and Todd agreed.

Coda sat behind his desk and lit a pipe, waving the match to put out the flame and dropping the stick in a small ashtray.

The window off to his left, the glass extra thick to shield him from sniper fire, looked out on the mountain, cable car, and part of the city beyond. If he had looked closely enough, he might have seen the roof of Dane's safe house.

Coda puffed on the pipe. He raised his head as the office door opened and his lieutenant, Sergio Varga, entered.

Varga looked out of shape with his barrel-chested build, but Mother Nature had made him that way. He was solid muscle underneath. He concealed his physique with loose clothing; he wore white slacks and a yellow shirt with the top button undone. The shirt was long enough to conceal the pistol he always wore on his right hip.

"What is it, Sergio?"

"A report from an army patrol arrived a few minutes ago, Ramon."

"And?"

"Last night they found a stray parachute outside the city. Prior to that, a spotter saw a landing beacon. That's what made them go look."

"What did they find?"

"Only the parachute."

Coda nodded and let out a stream of smoke scented with rum. "Could be Stone's friends."

"One, at least."

"Either we aren't looking hard enough, or they are just now arriving," Coda said. "Send more men to check around. Even the small neighborhoods. They could be anywhere."

Varga nodded and left his boss alone.

Coda sat quietly and smoked. Perhaps the arrival of Stone's friends worked in his favor. After all, he wouldn't have to go looking for them after executing Stone. They could instead all die together.

He laughed a little.

Chapter Five

McConn opened a large sea bag and began laying weapons on the living room carpet. "Here's what we have."

Dane already had his personal pistol, the Detonics Scoremaster .45 auto, and Nina her 9-millimeter Smith & Wesson. The heavy weapons from the sea bag were welcome additions.

McConn set out three AK-12s, along with the RPG-7 shoulder-fired grenade launcher. They spent a half-hour loading magazines to the tune of kids playing soccer outside, their laughter loud through the open windows. Dane didn't like the idea of innocent people so close to a battleground, but that was life in Colombia. They were probably more used to flying bullets than he was.

The thought angered him. He was spending his life trying to protect such people from aggressors they had no defense against. Having suffered his own tragedy in life, the suicide of his father and associated charges of treason against his country, there had been nobody to give Dane a hand when he needed one. Alleged friends had turned their backs on the family. He didn't want anybody else to suffer the same humiliation.

But there was only so much one man could do. Even if he had friends. The violence never ended. At least Dane had the means to try and stop the blood tide, but he could fight until an enemy finally struck him down and nothing much would have changed.

He wasn't dead yet, however, and he had the means to fight to the end, thanks to a cache of diamonds liberated from somewhere in Africa. The owner of a diamond mine had hired Dane's mercenary battalion to protect the property; instead, Dane found out about his criminal activities that included human trafficking. Dane shot the man and took off with as much of the loot as he could carry.

The new owners, grateful to Dane for getting rid of a very bad man, also provided funds when asked. He very rarely had to charge anybody for his services.

The three finished loading the weapons and returned them to the sea bag. McConn carried the bag down to the SUV and placed it in the back, covering it with a blanket.

As he shut the tailgate, a black GM SUV stopped at the end of the street and two men climbed out.

The kids noticed them too and began chanting, "*El cartel está aquí!*" "The cartel is here! The cartel is here!" The kids scattered for homes, and mothers called to stragglers.

The cartel goons started calling out to some of the mothers, "*Donde están los gringos?*" "Where are the gringos?" But the women closed doors in their faces. One straggling brat kid who probably wanted to join the cartel someday pointed toward the safe house.

"*Por allá, de allá!*"

McConn rushed up the steps. He met Dane and Nina in the living room, and they already had their pistols ready.

"We heard the kids," Dane said.

"Two men, no visible weapons, end of the block."

"Get the rest of the gear and I'll cover the front," Dane said.

Nina and McConn grabbed two more sea bags containing clothes and more equipment and hustled to the Chevy. Dane stepped out onto the outer deck, staying low in the doorway, the stainless Scoremaster .45 auto in his right hand.

The two cartel hoods stayed close to the house fronts, one of them holding a pistol.

Dane let them get a little closer.

A little closer.

Now!

"Hey, *muchachos*!"

They stopped short. Dane extended the .45 and fired twice. Flame flashed from the muzzle like lightning, and it struck down the ungodly without mercy. The first thug fell back into his partner, the second falling onto the sidewalk, but crawling clear of his partner and rolling into the street. Dane fired again and missed, the slug whining off the asphalt. The thug raised his own gun and Dane fired a fourth round. The .45 ACP hollow-point punched through the gunman's chest and pinned him to the street.

The Chevy SUV screeched out of the garage. Dane swung his legs over the deck railing and leaped onto the roof of the vehicle. Nina pushed open a back door and Dane swung inside.

McConn drove a little faster than normal but still kept the speed low as he went down the hill and made a left turn.

"This is an old man's getaway," Dane said.

"Change of plans?" Nina said.

"We can hit the house while they're looking for us," McConn said. "They'll send everybody out." Another turn.

He sped up a little more on the main drag.

Dane considered the idea. The estate had the perfect spot to land a chopper, they knew where Stone was, and McConn had a point.

Sometimes the simple plan was the best plan and they had to strike before circumstances reversed.

"I like it," Dane said. "Let's go look at the cable car."

They found a hiding spot in the brush surrounding the cable car station, having taken turns changing into combat gear in the back of the Chevy. They stayed behind the thick forest as the cable car rumbled down the line and stopped at the glass-enclosed switch house where two men operated a control panel. The cable car doors slid open and more troops filed out. Each cartel trooper held an automatic weapon. They piled into waiting SUVs and drove off. Once the engines had faded, only two troopers remained at the switch house, the armored sedan the only car still parked.

"Four guys per car," Dane said, "three cars. Twelve guys on the street looking for us. How many did you say were at the estate?"

"Twenty."

"So maybe seven guys left, give or take."

"Counting those two?"

"Let's say they're extra."

Nina tied back her hair. "I'm tired of talking. Can we start shooting already?"

"Will m'lady do the honors?" Dane said.

Nina placed her AK on the ground, took out her pistol and attached a silencer. She rested the barrel of the 9-millimeter on a log and waved Dane and McConn ahead.

Dane and McConn moved in as Nina fired twice. Glass shattered and the slugs punched through the heads

of the troopers. Dane and McConn entered the switch
house and threw levers to send the cable car up, McConn
holding the brake lever as Dane and Nina jumped in.
McConn let the brake go and leaped into the cable car
as it began to ascend. The forest enveloped them, and
they kept eyes ahead. The rooftop of Coda's mansion
appeared over the tops of the trees.

Chapter Six

Dane and Nina checked their AK-12s. McConn readied the RPG-7 rocket launcher. He had a satchel of spare rockets on his back. The cable car swayed in the wind, tree branches brushing and scraping against the metal side. The topside switch house loomed before them and they dropped low. A trooper at the top gazed curiously at the returning cable car but made no move for his weapon. He approached to investigate. When he came around the side, Dane blasted him into eternity, the AK popping loudly.

Dane, Nina and McConn ran out through the switch house and onto the estate property. The dirt courtyard had a large tree in the center. Somebody on an upper level of the house shouted. Dane and Nina sprayed covering fire while McConn raised the RPG. The rocket flashed from the tube and exploded through the window. Flame flashed through the upper level. An alarm began blaring. The fight was on. No turning back. McConn reloaded as three troopers came around one corner.

Dane and Nina broke for the adobe shed, gunfire splitting the air around them. McConn fired the second rocket, the corner of the house exploding. Fire and debris wiped out the three gunmen, the explosion covering their screams. McConn fired a third rocket at the upper window of Coda's office, but the blast only carved a chunk out of the thick glass. Chunks of the outer wall fell into the courtyard. McConn dropped the RPG and shouldered his AK. Time to finish this the old-fashioned way.

Sergio Varga, Coda's lieutenant, tossed his boss an Uzi from the wall safe. Coda took cover near his desk. When the RPG hit the window, the blast tore out a portion of the glass and ripped holes in the masonry. Fire from the rocket spread inside and licked at the ceiling. Smoke began filling the room. But the window held. It didn't mean they were safe, but they had more time to get away. And time was more valuable than gold.

Automatic gunfire crackled below. Varga ran to the door and peeked out.

"Clear!" he said. Coda joined him and they slipped into the hallway, avoiding the straight-ahead route to the stairs, where three of his troops waited, and instead taking the section of the hall that branched off to the right.

McConn entered the foyer, dodging left as three more gunmen fired from the top of the stairs. He dived to the floor and slid across the smooth wood to a doorway, crawling into the library to lean out. The troopers started down. McConn held the AK tight as the recoil kicked against him, stitching the troopers through chests and throats, stray slugs tearing up the wall.

McConn stepped over the bodies and took the steps two at a time. At the top landing, he dropped low and stayed close to the banister. Coda and another man broke to the right. McConn triggered a burst and the man with Coda screamed, crashing to the floor. McConn dived as Coda's Uzi chewed up the banister. The shooting stopped and McConn ran after the cartel boss, clearing the turn as Coda hustled down some steps. Coda tried to turn and fire but doing so on the steps caused him to lose his balance. His shots went wide. He landed on the ground hard, losing his grip on the Uzi. The submachine gun slid across the floor.

McConn ran down the steps. Coda screamed and crawled for the Uzi. McConn reached the gun first and kicked it away, the weapon smacking into a wall to spin off in another direction. Coda looked wide-eyed at McConn.

"So long, tubby," McConn said, and filled Coda with lead, the bright flash from the muzzle filling the space. McConn reloaded and continued through the house. He didn't give the drug thug's body a second glance.

Dane and Nina followed a path to the adobe shed. They heard the horses, their nervous breathing and snorting growing louder as they approached.

"Don't shoot the horses," Dane said.

"I won't shoot the horses," she said.

They reached the entryway, Dane on one side and Nina on the other. A last scan showed no threats, but a lot of smoke filled the courtyard. Dane eased around the corner with the AK out in front, and Nina followed.

Stone, on the wall, said, "Steve!"

Dane rushed over while Nina swung her weapon left, then right, and turned to watch the way from which they had come.

"I'm alone," Stone said.

"Who has the key?" Dane said.

"You probably blew him up," Stone said with a wince.

"Is that a thank you I heard?" Dane said.

"Idiots." Nina yanked a ring of skeleton keys from her web gear and tried three before she found one that unlocked Stone's shackles. Stone collapsed again.

"Can you run?" Dane said.

"I need a minute."

"We don't have a minute," Dane said.

"Incoming!" Nina said.

Two gunmen converged on the shed.

"Stay down, Dev!"

Nina opened fire on one side of the entryway, and Dane took the other. They traded shots with the gunmen, bullets smacking the adobe around them. The horses made more noise and smashed against the gate holding them in their part of the shed. Dane let the AK hammer against his shoulder, cutting through the foliage the gunmen were hiding behind. Dane and Nina fired at movement in the brush, one scream accompanying the shots.

"Here comes Todd!" Nina said.

McConn ran out of the front of the house, spotted the last trooper firing on the shed and aimed the AK while running. His salvo punched through the man's back. The cartel gunner cried out and fell. McConn reached the shed and frowned.

"Am I doing all the work?"

Dane and Nina supported Stone and carried him out. McConn took over while Dane pulled a satellite phone from his pack. He dialed quickly and spoke to the pilot of the chopper that had been pre-arranged by Stone's people. Dane told him they were ready for pickup and put the phone away.

"Who's flying?" Stone said.

"Sammy."

McConn and Nina moved forward with Stone between

them while Dane covered the rear with the sweeping muzzle of his AK-12.

The cable car shuddered to life and started down the hill.

"They're back!" Dane said.

"Double-time, come on!" McConn said. They moved out at a quick pace and crossed the edge of the property for the deep forest ahead.

Chapter Seven

Coda's troops unloaded from the cable car and stopped at the sight of the damaged house. The second-floor fire burned steadily, sending black and gray smoke skyward. Somebody entered the switch house to send the cable car back down for the next load while the rest of the squad started running for the landing area.

McConn hoisted Stone over his shoulders in a traditional fireman's carry so they could move faster. He ran in front of Dane and Nina, who watched the rear, as they tramped through the forest, weaving through the trees, fallen logs and natural debris, snapping twigs and branches and leaving heavy boot prints on the ground.

McConn breathed hard under the extra weight, but Stone couldn't walk or run.

"Not much further," Dane said.

"I don't hear the chopper," Nina said.

They plowed through the tree line to the clearing used for chopper landings and scoured the sky. No sign of any helicopter.

"Did you call them?" McConn said.

"You heard me call them!" Dane aid.

They cut left across the clearing to another tree line and found cover. Stone crawled to a spot near a tree and stayed flat. The others spread out.

Dane took out the satellite phone again and called the chopper, but there was no answer.

Nina's AK chattered as the cartel troops reached the clearing. McConn sprayed a pattern of fire along with her.

Dane dropped onto his belly. Return fire hammered their way, the thick brush making target identification tough for both sides. Not that Dane complained. He fired at movement, and a mist of blood signaled a hit. He fired again, saw nothing, and then a trooper stuck his rifle out too far. Dane gave him a burst. The trooper dropped backward. Dane sprayed a line of rounds at random, changed magazines and shouted, "I'm open to suggestions!"

A salvo from McConn's AK, cut down two cartel troopers trying to rush the clearing. As they fell, their compatriots shuffled positions, some exposing themselves. Dane fired with Nina and McConn, but the brush swallowed up the opposing force once again.

"Try the chopper again!" Stone shouted. "He has to be there now!"

Dane scooted back for more cover and called the pilot again. Still nothing.

Nina shouted, "Last mag!" as she reloaded.

Dane checked his mag pouch. Only one magazine left for him, too.

"I'm out!" McConn shouted.

The sat phone beeped. Dane tossed his mag to McConn and answered.

"Where the hell have you been?"

"Trying to avoid police choppers. Everybody's hauling ass to your location."

"We're under fire, get down here!"

"Coming in from the south. Throw smoke so we don't shoot you."

Dane moved close to the edge of the tree line. He tossed a smoke grenade that landed a few feet away. Red smoke hissed out and built a cloud in front of him and his team.

Dane dropped back as Nina and McConn ceased fire. The cartel troops responded to the ceasefire by breaking through the tree line. As they ran, the whipping rotor blades of the helicopter grew in volume and the chopper appeared over the trees, swinging perpendicular to the cartel troops.

A door gunner behind a .50-cal machine gun opened fire, hosing the line of troops. Some fell and others ran back for cover, only to get cut down on the second salvo.

Dane and Nina broke cover to run for the chopper while McConn carried Stone. Stray fire nicked at their heels but the thumping .50 kept the enemy pinned down.

Dane and Nina jumped aboard and helped McConn and Stone, and then the chopper lifted off. A few last bursts from the .50 offered their final goodbye to the cartel and Bogotá.

As the chopper rose over the trees, Dane and the gunner slammed the side doors and flopped onto the bench seats lining the front and back of the cabin.

"Where to now?" Stone asked.

"*Athena* just off the coast," Dane said. "Full steam to Crete."

"You think of everything," Stone said.

The freighter *Athena* chugged along the choppy Atlantic, a dull gray working ship with as many dings in the hull as official markings. It was part of Stone's fleet and had made many smuggling trips around the world with nary a suspicious glance from customs.

Inside, in a cabin, Steve Dane stepped out of the shower and dried off. Nina lay on the bed in a bathrobe.

Dane pulled his clothes on again. They were dirty from the fight and smelled of dry sweat and smoke.

"What are you doing?" Nina said.

"Checking on Dev."

"The doctor said he's fine."

"I'll just be a minute."

"Come to bed."

Dane shut the cabin door and went aft to the sick bay. The bearded doctor looked up from his desk.

"Can I see him?"

"He's sleeping."

Dane crossed the room to another doorway where the beds were. Devlin Stone lay with the covers up to his neck, unconscious, tubes plugged into his wrists and a heart monitor beeping steadily.

"What kind of shape is he in?" Dane said.

"Cuts and abrasions. Dehydration. He needs rest."

"Thanks, Doc."

Dane returned to the cabin and shut off the light. Nina was under the covers with the bathrobe on the floor. He undressed and slid under the covers. It was a tight fit. The bed had not been made for two. They had to share a pillow.

"Where are we going now that the shooting is over?" she said, snuggling against him.

"South of France," he said. "Maybe Monaco."

"Why?"

"Why not? I can't remember the last time we visited."

"You just want to gamble your money away."

"Um, usually that's *your* job, dear."

"Why don't we just relax at home for a change?"

Dane didn't reply.

"Duh," she said, scratching nails down his chest. "What a silly question."

He nudged her and she rolled on top of him.

A week later, with Stone up and around, the *Athena* docked at Crete. Dane, Nina, McConn and Stone stood by the starboard railing as the tugboats pushed the ship into port. The wind carried the faint scent of salt water.

"We're heading for Italy next," Stone said. "Gonna stick around?"

"I will," McConn said.

"Not us," Dane said. "On to the next adventure."

"You don't know when to stop, do you?"

"I'll stop when I'm dead."

"Nobody ever asks my opinion," Nina said.

Customs came aboard to check out the ship and clear Dane's and Nina's entry. Shortly after, Stone and McConn escorted Dane and Nina down the plank to the dock.

"I can't thank you enough," Stone said.

"You're always there when I call," Dane said. "Least I could do."

"We'll do something again soon, I imagine."

"Bet on it."

They shook hands and said good-bye, Stone and McConn getting a hug from Nina. She and Dane started across the busy shipyard. Trucks rumbled here and there; long cranes unloaded ships; loud voices carried with the wind.

"We should go home first," he said, "and pack a few things."

"Good idea. Unlike you, I refuse to wear the same underwear every day."

"I don't do that."

"You're a liar."

"And you're a drama queen."

"That's as close to true royalty as I'll ever get."

Chapter Eight

John Blaze drew the sheet up over his naked body and watched the countess emerge from the bathroom. She was a looker, all right. Long dark hair fell in a curly wave down her back. Big brown eyes and long elegant fingers that smoothed a short red negligee with nothing underneath that highlighted her creamy white skin. She stood in the doorway with hands on hips, legs slightly apart, the negligee draped over her slim frame. She cocked her head and smiled.

"You like, *Sir* John?"

He smiled back, his own upper-class British accent matching the woman's. "What's not to like?"

Countess Louisa Fromme grinned. She had a small mouth so it wasn't a wide grin, since Blaze didn't like women with mouths large enough to swallow a Ford F-150. Countess Louisa was the perfect companion for this particular visit to the Riviera: married, and unhappy.

And she'd fallen for the charms of Sir John Baker, who claimed to be the oldest son of a British industrial tycoon and had a crap ton of money to throw around.

Of course, he wasn't all he claimed. His family had

indeed christened him John, but he'd never received the knighthood, and his name wasn't Baker, and his real father had been an electrician, not a mogul of any sort. His mother had taught school. Both were gone now. Blaze, their only child, had no other family.

Sometimes that bothered him. It would have been nice to have some sort of port to call home, but his situation allowed him to wander the world at will. Nobody to check in with. Nobody to tell him to grow up.

The countess crawled across the bed, the front of the negligee falling open, and plopped onto her back. She put her hands behind her head. "Show me you can do this better than my husband. Or my last three lovers."

"Challenge accepted."

Two hours later, Countess Louisa lay under the sheet, curled up, sound asleep. She'd rolled off of him after three rounds without giving a verdict. Perhaps the jury was still out.

Blaze, naked, stood by the patio windows looking at the ocean in the distance. Or at least in that direction. There was no moon, so he couldn't see even a hint of the water.

He let out a breath that fogged a spot on the glass. She wasn't bad as conquests go, but not much fun, either. He didn't even care what the verdict was. His visit to the Riviera was supposed to be relaxing, but he felt a restlessness that wouldn't go away.

The authorities weren't chasing him, no unfortunate victim of his trade coming after his head. What was keeping him awake was boredom. He needed a new challenge. Something exciting. Worse, he knew it was all a matter of waiting for the phone to ring.

His cell phone, buried in a trouser pocket, started to chime as if on cue. The trousers lay in a pile next to the bed with the rest of his clothes. He knelt to retrieve the phone, pressing "Answer" to cut off the ring. Countess Louisa didn't stir.

Blaze said, "Yes?"

"Mr. Blaze," the caller, male, said, "we need you."

His pulse quickened. Now he was going to have some *real* action. The countess could piss off. "Where?"

"There's a car waiting downstairs."

"On the way."

Blaze hung up, quickly dressed, and slipped out of the room without waking the countess.

The lobby of the Royal Riviera contained only the cleaning crew at this late hour. Even the fellow pushing a vacuum across the red carpet and a woman dusting picture frames on the marble-white walls wore fancy uniforms. Top class, this place, but still boring. Blaze crossed the lobby to the exit with hurried steps. Excited steps.

To the average tourist on the Riviera, John Blaze was another young playboy spending the family fortune. To the police of the E.U., he was a wanted thief. Nothing penny-ante, either. He went after art, jewels, the treasures of the rich. They were easy targets and offered the biggest rewards along with the lowest risks.

And when he wasn't thieving, he worked odd jobs for a group of retired intelligence professionals called The Trust, represented by his recent caller. If asked, he'd admit his work for them was ten times better than ripping off necklaces from people like the Countess or forging a Rembrandt. That stuff was child's play. With The Trust, he took on bad guys that made him look like a saint.

He stepped out into the crisp nighttime air, his shoes scraping the steps as he hustled down to a waiting limousine. He hopped in the back. The driver pulled away before Blaze closed the door. He settled into the plush seat. The limo's insulation made it a quiet ride. Streetlights flashed through the tinted windows.

"'Bout a ten-minute drive, sir," said the driver over the intercom.

"Enough time for a spot of this excellent brandy," Blaze said. He took bottle and glass from a mounted tray and poured two fingers. Then he sat back and let the brandy warm his stomach.

The Trust didn't call often. In fact, this was his first contact with them in over fourteen months.

Blaze was sure the call was worth the wait.

Late-hour traffic made the ride longer than ten minutes. The anticipation of his pending assignment made it hard to sit still. His right foot kept tapping on the carpet.

The three men who made up The Trust had literally snatched him off the street several years ago. He'd thought his free rein had finally come to an end, but the big men in black who had collected him were definitely not cops. Had some of his victims hired the muscle? What sort of grave awaited him? He'd found himself very calm about the snatch. The day had to come, eventually. He knew it always would. It was the fine print of a contract he had signed with Fate long ago.

He'd been deposited in a penthouse suite instead of a shallow grave and the three men of The Trust made their offer. They were retired intelligence officers who now ran their own organization. The battle against enemies of freedom never ended, and sometimes Western governments were hampered by diplomatic considerations and red tape. The delays allowed bad guys to flourish. The Trust sought to reverse that trend. They had no red tape to consider. They wanted Blaze on their team. Now and then they would call with an assignment and expected him to respond. In exchange, they'd provide him the necessary cover to operate as he saw fit.

Blaze decided he was a lucky man indeed and accepted. His fun was just beginning.

The limo driver stopped in front of a darkened restaurant, and he used a key to enter. He led Blaze to a back room lit by an overhead lamp. The three men of The Trust sat around a table. One of them dismissed the driver. Another offered Blaze an empty chair.

Blaze sat and looked at the weathered and elderly faces of the three men, each one of them in their late 70s. He didn't know their names. They were One, Two and Three, American, and they paid on time. Blaze hadn't bothered to give them silly nicknames, either.

"Thank you for joining us, Mr. Blaze," said Number One. "Did we get you out of bed?"

"Somebody's," Blaze said.

Number Two chuckled while Number Three remained silent. Number One shook his head. Blaze felt oddly chastised.

"I'd rather be here talking to you fellows," Blaze said quickly. "Where am I going this time?"

Number Two, directly across from Blaze, produced a manila envelope. He opened it and passed a photograph across the table.

Blaze examined the face of a man in his 60s. He wore a rumpled business suit and was walking down a busy street.

Number One, "That is Mr. Theodore Trent. Spent decades as an engineer and now he runs a company selling equipment to the United States military."

Blaze nodded.

"Mr. Trent has run into hard times. His latest project, a

direct energy weapon, or DEW, was rejected by the US in favor of a competitor with a superior design."

"Whoa," Blaze said. "A laser gun? Like *Star Wars*?"

"Eventually," Number One said, "but right now the technology is still in the infant stages. The DEW emits concentrated energy on a target, but the beam is invisible and must be held on the target for a period of time before the target is destroyed. But the weapon works."

"If you were shooting at an enemy tank," said Blaze, "it sounds as if the enemy would have time to adjust its turret and shoot first."

"Yes, but that won't be the case forever."

"Is Trent out to sabotage the competition?"

"No. He's invested millions of dollars and needs to recoup that. He has approached another buyer."

"China?"

"The Russians," said Number One.

"Not a crime, is it? The Cold War is long over."

"If this were about maintaining the status quo, a balance of power, we'd let the sale go through. But I don't have to remind you that Vladimir Putin has made some very aggressive moves lately. Russia's failing infrastructure includes its military and he needs all the help he can get."

Number Three continued. "And we can't let him get his hands on this weapon."

"It's probably a bit big to steal," Blaze said.

"You are not being asked to steal it," Number One said. "It must be destroyed, but we have other people in mind for that. Your job is very specific. Trent will be meeting a Russian representative named Arkady in Monaco, not far from here. The meeting takes place in three days. Trent plans to show Arkady technical specifications to whet their appetites. We want you to steal those technical documents.

By the time Trent returns home, the second phase will also be completed and the weapon destroyed. We want no trace of this *laser gun* left in existence. Good luck, Mr. Blaze. Our driver will return you to the hotel."

"All right."

"Do you have any questions?"

"None," Blaze said. "I already have an idea of how to get those documents."

"You're the expert," said Number One. "That's why we recruited you."

Blaze helped himself to more brandy on the way back. He returned to find the Countess still sound asleep. Her romp with him had really knocked her cold. Dropping his clothes in a pile once more, he climbed back into bed. She shifted and wrapped warm legs around him.

He might as well stick around long enough to hear the verdict, but after that, he'd begin the new adventure and leave the countess to her misery.

Chapter Nine

Nina Talikova sat at a baccarat table under bright lights and beside painted arches in the main room of the Casino de Monte-Carlo. She wore a tight-fitting blue party dress with gold earrings and black stilettos. A cocktail waitress stepped beside her, removing her empty glass and replacing it with a full vodka tonic. It was her fourth.

"Mademoiselle? Your bet?"

Nina stared at the small stack of plaques in front of her with little comprehension.

She looked up lazily at the banker across the table.

"I'm sorry, how much?" She spoke slowly so as not to slur.

"Five million." The banker held disapproval in his dark eyes, but Nina didn't flinch. If she wanted to be looked at with derision, she'd have remained in Moscow with her so-called family.

Nina counted her stack. Ten million. She took the bet and placed half the stack near the center of the table.

The players on her left, a gray-haired older couple, passed on the bet, so Nina faced the banker alone.

The banker slipped four cards from the shoe, a box containing six well-shuffled packs of cards. The croupier next to the banker used a long wooden spatula to pass Nina's two cards to her.

The heavyset older woman bundled in a heavy blue suit shot Nina yet another death glare of disapproval. It was beginning to be a thing around the table. Nina figured they'd all calm down if they had a drink or two of their own.

"That's your fourth drink," she said. "You should really take it easy."

An American, Nina noticed. Stupid do-gooder. Americans traveling abroad always seemed to think people wanted to hear the rot coming out of their mouths, as if their First Amendment rights made it a requirement that they talk a lot, for a long length of time, and never said anything of substance.

Nina noted that along with the suit, the woman wore shiny gold and diamond rings on almost every finger. Another trait of Americans. Big show offs.

Nina decided to go nuclear and shut her down for good. "I'll stop drinking," she said, "when you drop 50 pounds. Deal?"

The woman gasped.

Nina slowly turned her head away from the woman and examined at her cards. *That should keep her quiet.* She held a jack of hearts and an ace of spades. The ace gave her one point; the jack, like all face cards in baccarat, held zero value. She had to get as close as she could to nine in three cards or less.

The banker showed his cards and Nina's score didn't matter. Nine of clubs and jack of diamonds. A natural. Nina tossed her cards at the croupier, who shifted her plaques to the banker's side.

With a snort and a glare, the heavyset woman and her younger female companion left the table. Nina looked over her shoulder at their departing backs and stuck out her tongue.

She turned back to see the smoldering stares of the banker and croupier.

Nina smiled smartly and gulped her drink. *Where was Steve?*

The banker offered his next bet at eight million francs. Nina passed. Some spectators and the remaining two players contributed enough to make the bet. The spectators split between betting on who would win, the bankers or the players.

Nina and her fuzzy brain had had enough. It was after midnight. She tipped the croupier, who didn't say thank you, and grabbed her vodka tonic along and plaques and departed. She marched toward the bar on the other side of the room and found a stool. She sat with her back straight. She wasn't going to slouch in public.

It was a nice hotel, Nina had to admit. The arched ceilings were painted in a homage to, or rip-off of, the Sistine Chapel; similar paintings lined the walls, each corner of the paintings impeccably lined up with its neighbor.

She took a long drink, tipping back her head, and almost fell off the stool. She decided to stand up and instead lean against the bar. Classier that way. Two nearby Frenchmen talked football, with one glancing in her direction. She caught the look in her peripheral vision. Took another drink. The man who examined her wore a tux and bow tie. He interrupted his pal mid-thought to rise from the chair and come over to her. She leaned toward him and spoke before the man opened his mouth. "*Vous êtes une grenouille degoutant.*"

The man blinked in surprise, muttered something and went back to his pal, who laughed.

"Be nice," a man over her shoulder said. Steve Dane eased onto the stool next to her. He wore a tux with a loose bow tie. "Really, you had to call him a disgusting frog?"

"I almost," she said, "told him in Russian."

"How did you do?"

"Never mind that. Where have you been?"

"That fish didn't sit well with me."

"Awwww, your tummy upset?"

"And any rats in the sewers are in for a bad night."

The bartender came over and Dane ordered a martini. "Don't forget the vermouth," he said. The bartender nodded dutifully and filled a shaker. Dane watched the bartender stir the gin and vermouth and gladly accepted the offered glass.

"How did you do?" Dane asked again.

Nina opened her purse and placed the four plaques on the bar.

Dane whistled. "The money will dry up someday, you know. We should try and save a little."

"I saw a rich American bitch we can hustle," Nina said. "I'm sure she's a criminal."

"Nina—"

"Especially in that suit."

"Nina, what's wrong?"

"I am bored, Steve. B-O-R-E-D." She slurred as she spelled the word. "This was a stupid idea."

"We've only been here a few days," Dane said. "Something will turn up."

"Right now, only your stomach is turning up."

"Turning over, actually." Dane grabbed his drink and the four plaques. "Come on, let's find another game."

Dane noticed the two Frenchmen glaring at them as they departed.

"You hurt his feelings, dear," Dane said.

She spat a curse in Russian.

"Let's go find that fat lady and steal her rings."

"Now, now, dear."

Chapter Ten

Dane traded the plaques for chips at the roulette table.

"You realize you're playing Russian with a roulette?"

"Want to rephrase that, honey?"

She laughed and swallowed more of her drink. Dane held the martini in his left hand while he placed chips on the table with his right. He covered a spread of numbers.

Other players placed their bets, and then the wheelman spun the wheel and dropped the ball.

The table was a European single-zone, as one would expect, and the wheel rotated in an ornate wooden base. The ball traveled counter-clockwise to the wheel, riding in a raised groove.

Dane watched the table, second-guessing his spread. He felt a tension in his belly that had nothing to do with the fish.

Nina's eyes stayed with the ball until she had to grab the edge of the table to keep from falling over.

"You're running low on vitamins," he told her.

"Bottoms up," she said, and took another swallow.

The ball dropped from the groove and landed on

black eight. The wheelman called out the winners and passed them their chips. Dane did not collect any. He shook his head.

"You're having the same luck as me," Nina said. "Maybe we should bet on your next visit to the toilet instead."

Dane placed another spread on the table, a split between reds and blacks.

A new player joined as one couple departed. He exchanged plaques for chips and placed a short stack on red 71.

He wore a tux like Dane's, a Rolex on his left wrist, and had slicked blonde hair. Nina frowned and examined his face further. A thought tried to break through the vodka fog in her head.

The blonde man did not notice her.

Nina finished her drink and crunched an ice cube. Dane raised an eyebrow. She ignored him.

The wheel spun and the ivory ball began its hypnotic counter-roll.

The blonde player watched the ball with hands in his pockets. A waitress asked if he wanted to order, but he waved her off.

Nina tried to grab the thought in the back of her mind.

Something about…*the Rolex!*

The blonde fellow had no other distinguishing features. He wasn't bad looking, but he was also from central casting. Could have been anybody. Instead of a detriment, his ability to blend in was the secret of his success. He could have been a good spy, Nina once thought, but he became an excellent thief instead.

John Blaze, in the flesh. She never thought she'd see him again.

As a former agent of the Russian FSB, Nina had crossed paths with John Blaze once before, when the thief had

entered Moscow to steal something or other from one of
Putin's oligarch pals. She never discovered which item in
the rich man's dacha Blaze wanted. Nina and her team of
agents had foiled his robbery attempt before he reached the
home, but he'd slipped through their dragnet despite what
she thought had been a secured perimeter.

Blaze had sent a postcard to the FSB office shortly after.
Better luck next time, fools.

She had to admire his attitude if nothing else.

The ivory ball dropped onto red 71.

The other players congratulated the blonde man as his
short stack grew larger with the winnings. He tipped the
wheelman, cashed in and smiled as he left the table.

"He knows when to quit," said Dane. "I'd better take
a lesson."

Dane cashed out as well, and he and Nina wandered
across the casino to the patio doors, where they joined
other guests in the fresh air. The ocean sparkled under
the moonlight.

Nina smiled.

"What?"

"That blonde player. Something just turned up."

"Should I have recognized him?"

"He's a thief named John Blaze. Englishman. Likes
high-end jobs, art and jewels, that sort of thing. He once
tried to rob an oligarch in Moscow. We almost caught him."

"But he slipped through the net."

"It was a draw," she said. "He didn't get away with
anything either."

Dane pulled her close. "And what are you thinking?"

"He's probably here on a job. It would be fun to see
what he's up to."

"Nina—"

"Steve, I'm so—"

"B-O-R-E-D. I heard you. There might be a reward for his capture. We could use the money after tonight."

"True. Let's talk more about it tomorrow. We should go back to the room and see if we can get lucky another way."

Dane didn't argue.

John Blaze visited the cashier to trade his chips for cash and took the stairs to one of the casino's restaurants, where he ordered a late dinner, grilled salmon with asparagus. He paged through a small notebook, sipping water with a lemon wedge, while he waited. The notebook contained his initial brainstorms for the Trent operation.

He always worked alone, so nobody accompanied him. He'd passed the Countess's test, and she'd been eager for another bout after tending to some business with her husband, but he had to let her down with his sudden departure. Business of the crown, he'd told her, and her confusion about what that meant still amused him.

The waiter brought his meal and refilled the water glass. He put the notebook away. The fish and asparagus needed no knife. His fork cut through both. After this he'd spend a little more time in the casino before hitting the rack for the night. He had another twenty-four hours to learn the layout of the casino and neighboring hotel, where Trent and the Russian would meet.

Twenty-four hours to create a plan to steal documents for a laser weapon. He'd have felt silly thinking about such things if it wasn't real.

The heater of the Mercedes S-Class sedan warmed the inside well enough, but Alexander Arkady still wore a heavy coat. Another cold day in Moscow. He sipped a flask full of hot coffee rather than vodka.

The Mercedes traveled down Simonovskaya nab, presently connecting with Vostochnay nab and passing drab buildings jammed together in a tight cluster. The driver stopped in front of a tall brick building across from empty tennis courts. Too cold to play. Not even the most dedicated tennis player wanted to brave the chill. The driver shut off the motor.

Arkady was not alone in the sedan.

Two FSB officers rode with him, one up front with the driver and the other in back with him. Arkady and the two cops exited the vehicle. Their breath formed clouds as they walked up the entrance steps to the apartment. One of the FSB officers held the door for Arkady, who entered without pause.

Tall, thin, with a partially bald head and a narrow nose that hooked slightly downward, Arkady resembled a hawk, so that's what he was known as: "the Hawk." The man who swooped down to do Putin's dirty work when the targets of such dirty work least expected.

The entryway had dirty white walls and stained tiles. Mailboxes covered either side of the walls. Arkady and his men bypassed the elevator, which probably didn't work, and started up the stairs, pushing aside a young couple exiting the stairwell. The male half almost raised his voice until a glare from the FSB men ended whatever he was about to say. He urged his female companion down the steps and away from the men.

Some things in Russia never changed.

The heavy boots Arkady and the FSB men wore clunked loudly as they marched up the stairs to the third floor. One of the FSB agents held the hallway door while Arkady followed the frayed brown carpet to an apartment midway down the hall.

The FSB men unzipped their coats to draw MP-443 Grach 9-millimeter pistols, which they held beside their legs. Arkady raised a fist to pound on the door. Then he stepped back to let one of the FSB kick the door open. The door crashed inward, slamming against the inner wall, one hinge coming loose from the frame. Arkady and the FSB marched inside.

The apartment wasn't large, and the front door opened on a living room with a kitchenette. An older man in shabby clothes and uncombed gray curly hair sat at a table against the wall, spoonful of stew halfway to his mouth. He stared with wide eyes as Arkady approached. The FSB officers, their Grach pistols well in view, spread out. But the older man's eyes did not leave Arkady's.

Arkady spoke in a low voice. "Georgi Koskov, you are under arrest for the possession of illegal drugs."

Koskov dropped his spoon, a spray of stew dotting his shirt. "You're mad, Arkady." He rose. "There are no drugs in this apartment, only a man who will not abide by the madness of your precious Putin! And tell your *thugs* to put away their guns! Have some respect!"

Arkady gestured with his left hand, and the FSB officers holstered the pistols. They quickly searched the room, turning over sofa cushions, knocking books off shelves, making a racket and a mess.

Koskov watched with unblinking despair. Arkady sipped coffee from his flask.

Koskov turned from the FSB men to Arkady. "You cannot do this. There are no drugs here. Unless you planted them. You're arresting me because of my *articles*! Your master won't tolerate dissent!"

"Stop talking, Georgi."

"You're taking us backward and ruining the Motherland! You're going to start a war!"

One of the FSB returned from the bedroom. He held up a bag of white powder for the Hawk to see, but Arkady didn't even give the officer a glance.

"Such a shame, Georgi."

The color drained from Koskov's face as the other FSB officer locked handcuffs around the writer's wrists, wrenching the man's arms behind his back. Koskov winced.

"Gently," Arkady said. "He's older."

Koskov cursed Arkady as the officers led him out. The curses grew in volume as the men headed down the hallway.

Arkady looked around at the mess and the wrecked door. Koskov's neighbors could pick out whatever they wanted, should they be so inclined. He turned on a heel and followed after his FSB escorts. He had another meeting soon. With Vladimir Putin himself.

Chapter Eleven

Squashed between Arkady and one of the FSB men in the back of the Mercedes, a thoroughly demoralized and subdued Koskov made no further protests as they traveled to FSB headquarters. Once they arrived, the two FSB officers unloaded Koskov and escorted him inside. Arkady settled back with a sigh and a sip of coffee as the driver merged with traffic once again and drove to the Kremlin.

As he watched the center of Russian government grow in the distance, Arkady could not help but reflect on Koskov's words. Putin had made no secret since day one of his presidency that he wished for a Russia restored to its glory days. No doubt eyes and ears in the West were watching as well. But Putin had the young people of Russia seeing the virtue in the old ways. Deals were being made to bring valued hard currency back into the economy. Koskov's voice of dissent stood in the way. Now, he'd be an example to others to shut up. Arkady knew it wouldn't be that easy, and he'd be planting much more evidence in the days, weeks, and months to come, because, for now, such arrests needed a cover story.

But the people would know what was happening. They would know that true leadership sat at the helm of the Kremlin once again.

Koskov's rants in the press would be judged to be those of a paranoid cocaine addict, and that worked to Putin's advantage.

The majestic white stone building of the Kremlin sat larger than life outside his window. The driver stopped for the guards at the gate. Arkady powered down his window so the armed soldier could see his face. He handed over his ID which the soldier examined and handed back. The driver drove on and parked in a reserved spot with other sedans, mostly Mercedes vehicles, in the neighboring spaces. The German company had recently built a factory in Russia to produce the cars for the government. They were a huge improvement over the ZIL sedans of old and signaled a resurgence in the government. There was money to spend. Money meant power, progress, and hope. Hope for a stronger Motherland. Hope for a return to Russian dominance in the world.

Arkady stepped out before the driver could open his door. He required no escort from this point.

He walked toward the entrance as his driver lit a cigarette.

Putin's assistant, a young man in a black suit, greeted Arkady in the outer office. He knocked on a connecting door, opened it far enough to stick his head in and announced Arkady's arrival.

Vladimir Putin's deep voice boomed from the other side of the door. "Send him in."

The assistant escorted the Hawk inside. The wood floor was covered with a thick roll of carpet, gray, with layered curtains over the windows. Bookcases lined the walls, with a sitting area on the opposite side of Putin's oakwood desk, which was spotless with a polished sheen. Golden eagles from the czarist regime sat atop another case. Putin rose and greeted Arkady with a hearty handshake.

"Welcome, Alexander."

"Good morning, sir."

Putin, wearing his own dark suit with loosened tie, guided Arkady to the sitting area. Arkady took a seat on a leather couch. Putin's assistant poured coffee into espresso cups and brought the cups to both men. The coffee let off wisps of steam. The cups were emblazoned with a small illustration of the Russian flag. Putin dismissed his assistant, who shut the office door behind him, sealing the two men in a comfortable but silent tomb.

"I asked you to come here for an important reason, Alexander," Putin said. "Operation Nightshade."

Arkady sipped his coffee. "I've read the file."

"We're going forward. Trent came to us, which is more than we could have asked, after he lost his bid with the US government to a competing company. When you go to the US to see Trent's prototype, I need the competing company's weapon destroyed."

Arkady raised an eyebrow.

"It would be nice if Trent could be blamed for the destruction," Putin said. "We need not dispose of him ourselves. Let the American authorities do that."

"Some would say such action—"

"Is an act of war, yes. I'm well aware. That's why Trent needs to, as the Americans say, take the fall."

Arkady started to speak. Putin held up a hand.

"We *are* at war, Alexander. And whether we want to admit it or not, as we continue our efforts here, the world will oppose us. The *Americans* will oppose us. They oppose us *now*. In acquiring Trent's laser weapon, we have the opportunity to gain an upper hand. We need to make sure the Americans suffer a setback. A scandal. While they prosecute Trent and sort out the mess, we surge ahead."

Arkady said, "He expects to sell the weapon, sir. Am I supposed to buy it?"

Putin waved him off. "Steal it, Alexander. I'm not paying forty million dollars for something we can just take."

"All of what you describe requires special assistance, sir."

"Of course. What do you need?"

"A ship. And Marco Cavallos."

Putin cracked half a grin. "You've been thinking about this."

Arkady sipped some more coffee.

"Why not our people, Alexander?"

"Cavallos has the connections and the skills."

"He's wanted by how many governments?"

"And he's managed to avoid capture in spite of that," Arkady said. "There's nobody better."

Putin nodded. "You will have him. A direct energy weapon will give us a tremendous edge in the days to come. Of course, if you are caught or killed—need I say more?"

"No, sir. It will be an honor to achieve this, Mr. President."

"Alexander. You can use the other word. Better days are coming."

"It will be an honor to achieve this," Arkady repeated, adding, "*Comrade* Putin."

The thirtysomething couple stepped off the elevator and the male half kept an arm around his wife. She used a key card and they entered their room. The wife went into the bathroom while the husband removed a rectangular device from the drawer where he'd lined up his socks.

Marco Cavallos turned on the device and started a circuit of the room, corner to corner: the lamps, under the bed and table, the window frame, the picture frames hanging on the walls. The green light on the device never turned red. There were no surveillance devices in the room.

The toilet flushed and presently Roxana came out. "Okay?"

Cavallos nodded. Roxana went into the closet and took out a briefcase, which she brought over to the writing table.

The couple looked completely normal, Marco with his olive skin, dark eyes and sharp jawline. He kept his hair cut short. He might have been a Telemundo soap star, or a truck driver. Born in Venezuela, he had long ago trained himself to speak without any hint of an accent.

"Have some coffee sent up while I change," Roxana said. She left the table to collect pajamas from the dresser and went into the bathroom once again.

Cavallos called room service for the coffee, then set about unpacking the briefcase. He unfolded a map and spread it on the table. He then placed glossy photographs also taken from the briefcase around the map. There was a red circle in the center of the map.

Roxana emerged wearing pink pajamas. She tied on a bathrobe and joined her husband. Even under the layers you could see the swell of her hips and get a hint of a small frame. She wore her hair short like her husband, but with blonde streaks in the brown locks. Her wedding ring contained a big diamond. She called it her own personal Rock of Gibraltar. She was French, her accent also gone, part of the price one paid to blend in while fighting for a cause nobody could remember anymore.

Now they just fought for themselves.

"Tomorrow's the day," she said.

"You secured the helicopter?"

"I did. You got the machine gun?"

"I did."

Room service knocked. Cavallos signed for the coffee and poured two mugs. Two sugar cubes for Roxana, black for him. They sipped the brew and stood over the map and pictures of HM Forest Bank, Manchester, off the Irwell River, and the place where the Crown had sent two al-Qaeda operatives caught in London.

Cavallos and his wife had been hired to break those prisoners out of the prison and return them to their brothers-in-arms. They hadn't agreed to the job straight away. First, they looked pictures of the prison. Second, they found the main weakness, which hadn't been hard, and was a testimony to the British and their flawed view of their invincibility. Third, they took the job. Now they were making final preparations for a mission that, without complications, would not only enrich their reputation, but also ruin the reputation of the Queen and her prison system.

The second accomplishment was a bonus that offered a great deal of amusement.

The map showed the countryside location of the prison. The photos were close-ups of the complex that Roxana had taken when they'd hiked the surrounding area.

Cavallos and Roxana traced the route they intended to fly. Up the Irwell, with a cut across Agecroft Cemetery, which would give them a straight shot at the prison.

The AQ operatives were housed, with the rest of the prisoners, on the north end of the property in a cluster of five buildings. Those buildings extended from a center circle like a windmill. Spaces between the buildings served as the exercise yards for the various wings, the prison's way of keeping the bulk of the population separate. They had to fly across the property, pepper a few selected spots with machine gun fire to create panic and land long enough to pick up the AQ operatives and whisk them to Scotland. In Scotland, they would hand over the former prisoners, ditch the helicopter and drive all the way back to London.

From London, they'd make their way wherever they wanted, though there was always, in the background, the threat of capture. The prices on both their heads totaled over two million US. If the authorities didn't catch them, there were plenty of bounty hunters willing to tangle.

Cavallos turned his thoughts back to the plan. Security at the prison was tight, the troopers assigned there well-armed, and a frontal assault was a good way to commit suicide. There was no way to break in and break out, but the prison had no defense against a chopper swooping in, picking up passengers, and flying away.

Roxana refilled her coffee mug. "What's our window?"

"Between noon and 12:15," Cavallos said. "We'll have no flexibility on this. Zero."

Roxana shrugged. "We've handled worse."

Cavallos and Roxana had met as members of the Basque underground in Spain, where they learned the tools of their trade. Engagements with Spanish authorities had tested them thoroughly, and they had managed to carry on while comrades fell. Able to make money on the freelance market, they now worked for various individuals and organizations that had horns instead of halos. It wasn't a bad life, but they had no real home or sanctuary. Always on the run, looking over their shoulders, one job to the next.

Such a life was exciting for a young person. They had once relished the idea of being a modern-day Bonnie &

Clyde, living by the gun as they'd surely die by the gun, but a funny thing happened on the way to leaving behind a good-looking corpse.

Ten years went by. Ten long years that had done more to fray their nerves than spike their adrenaline, and both were growing weary of the existence. They weren't ready to quit, not yet, but a home base, a place of security, a place of their own, would certainly be welcome.

When the AQ representatives had approached them about liberating their comrades, Cavallos had not only accepted, but based his resulting plan on a similar prison rescue in Canada. The perpetrators of that effort had been captured, but Cavallos figured out how not to make the same mistakes and, best of all, his plan had passed Roxana's critical eye.

"We can talk about this all night," he said, "but I think we need to get some rest."

"After the coffee? We'll be up for a while yet."

He smiled and pulled her to him. She looked up at him and bit her lower lip.

"What shall we do?" he said.

"We can think of something if we put our minds to it."

They did.

Chapter Twelve

The Huey helicopter sat in a private hangar that Roxana had rented for two months, cash paid in advance. She was halfway through her pre-flight check, one side panel of the chopper open so she could look at the oil level and examine the hoses, when Cavallos drove his car inside.

Turning off the motor, he exited to open the trunk and lift out a heavy item wrapped in a blanket. A steel tube with a vented muzzle attachment stuck out one end.

Roxana continued her pre-flight, moving down the fuselage to the tail rotor, while he unwrapped the US surplus M-60. The machine gun had a base stand with a rotating clamp. He placed the base inside the chopper cabin, making sure there was enough room to close the door with the weapon in place. Back to the car for a drill. Cavallos, with safety glasses over his eyes, proceeded to drill four holes in the cabin floor and lined the base up with the holes. With a power screwdriver, he bolted the base to the floor, then lifted up the M-60 and placed it on the rotating clamp. He tightened the clamp and tested the movement. It was a little stiff. A few drops of oil from Roxana's oil bottle corrected that problem, and then the M-60 moved freely in any direction Cavallos moved it.

Roxana finished and climbed into the cockpit. Cavallos tightened the bolts one more time and fed a cartridge belt into the M-60. Roxana said, "Five minutes."

Cavallos rotated the M-60 so it didn't extend out of the cabin, pulled the side door shut and jumped into the cockpit next to his wife. She fired up the rotors as he strapped in.

At full power the rotors created havoc inside the hanger, a hurricane of machine-generated wind that flung every scrap of debris into the air. Roxana lifted the Huey off the floor a few feet and eased the nose forward. She cleared the hangar door and traveled at a low hover across the blacktop.

They had chosen the private airfield outside Manchester because of its remote access and lack of control tower. A few private planes rested in other hangars, but it was more of a utility field than a regularly used airport. Roxana keyed her radio and announced to any air traffic in the area that she was lifting off. Another pilot replied that he was at 2,000 feet five miles south and would watch for her. Roxana acknowledged and raised the chopper off the ground and into the sky. At 3,000 feet she leveled off and steered north.

Lush green country ahead and underneath, with rolling hills and nary a strip mall in sight. The few white clouds hanging in the sky were no bother. Roxana's eyes continuously swept the instrument panel and the open space around the helicopter. The Huey could be seen on radar, but they had disabled the transponder, so any tower making contact would have no idea of their official identification. A major risk, but they wouldn't be airborne long.

Cavallos checked his watch. By now their client should

have sent word to the prisoners that they would soon be free, but it was the one part of the plan where he lacked control. If somehow the communication had failed, or been intercepted, the client should have let them know, but Cavallos knew he wasn't the only outlaw always looking over his shoulder. And the client had a place to hide.

Presently the Irwell River appeared on their right. Roxana steered that way. Over the river, she dropped to 1,500 feet. The ground rushed below them, and she followed each turn of the river, the Huey rocking side to side with each maneuver.

When Cavallos saw the cemetery ahead, he unbuckled and passed between the front seats to the rear cabin. He pulled on a headset with a microphone and asked if Roxana could hear him. She said yes. Opening the side door filled the cabin with a blast of warm air. Cavallos swung the M-60 out and cranked the charging handle.

The pivot point on the base still felt a little stiff. Cavallos moved the weapon up and down and back and forth, but despite the oil, it still wasn't ideal. Nothing he could do about it now except compensate for the problem, ie: really manhandle the weapon and shove the muzzle where he needed. There was no fear of breaking it. The hardened steel took more punishment with every exploding round than he could physically dish out.

Roxana cut left over a cemetery. The graveyard flashed below. Cavallos leaned out and saw the prison. He took aim. The M-60 bucked lightly against his shoulder, the stand taking most of the recoil. The first burst smacked into the main building. Random follow-up shots struck the guard towers, the administration offices, the dining hall. Return fire from the towers did no damage. The guards had only shotguns, and the pellets couldn't reach the Huey.

Roxana dropped low. Cavallos fired some more. The wail of the alarm didn't penetrate the roar of the chopper engines, but Cavallos could imagine it as he watched stray figures running for cover and into the closest building as the M-60 stingers rained down.

Roxana did one turn over the windmill of the cell blocks. Prisoners in orange jumpsuits scattered like so many ants, except for two who remained close to their building. Cavallos fired into the yard, the rounds tearing into the dirt and further holding back any approach. The two AQ prisoners broke into a sprint as Roxana set down. They might as well have been in slow motion, as every muscle in Cavallos's body tightened and he swung the M-60 to and fro looking for real targets. Then the two prisoners jumped into the cabin. Roxana lifted off. Guards in full tactical gear, with submachine guns now, ran out of one of the buildings. Their muzzles flashed. Rounds nicked the Huey. Cavallos triggered a stream of return fire in their direction. The response team scattered, but none appeared to fall to the 7.62x51mm NATO slugs. And then the Huey was out of range and climbing once again to 3,000 feet.

Cavallos faced the rescued men. Dark-skinned, short-haired, breathless. The orange jumpsuits had their numbers stenciled on the front. No names. Cavallos didn't mind that.

"We land again soon," he told them. They nodded and stayed back against the cabin wall.

Chapter Thirteen

Samin al-Bazr enjoyed the tranquility of the Scottish countryside with its rolling green hills, trees and gentle breeze. He took a deep breath. The fresh air felt crisp. This could be home someday, and then his watch beeped. Work intruded on tranquility.

He turned off the alarm and barked orders at his men. The two in the back seat of the Range Rover lumbered out, one carrying an empty RPG-7 while the other clutched a tote bag loaded with high-explosive projectiles. They ran across the field to a cluster of rocks.

Al-Bazr told the driver, "When you see the chopper, start the engine."

The driver, his eyes shielded by dark sunglasses, nodded.

Al-Bazr stepped out of the Rover to stand near the bumper. He held a briefcase for display only. The case was supposed to contain the balance of money owed to Cavallos and his wife. It was empty.

Presently the al-Qaeda operative heard the helicopter and scanned the sky. Then the chopper descended to the open field. The Rover's engine sparked to life.

Roxana dropped to 1,000 feet and went into a long circle over the open field. She saw the Rover, al-Bazr and his briefcase. She missed the rocks.

Cavallos didn't and said over the intercom, "Stay away from the rocks. Two men with a rocket launcher."

"What should we do?"

"Fly back over the field."

Roxana turned the chopper and Cavallos lunged at one of the prisoners, hitting him hard and grabbing a fistful of jumpsuit.

"Enjoy your virgins," he said to the screaming man as he flung the prisoner out the door. The man's arms and legs flailed as he fell like a rock. He landed headfirst.

The RPG-7 flashed from the rocks and the projectile zeroed in. Roxana pitched the chopper to the right, Cavallos grabbing the M-60 to keep from falling. Then the second prisoner was on him, pummeling with fists, wrenching off the headset. Cavallos struck back with an elbow that connected with the other man's chin. Cavallos turned and slammed a one-two combination into the prisoner's chest and stomach, then grabbed him by the belt and shoulder and threw him out for a short drop to the tranquil Scottish countryside.

The chopper rolled left as Roxana dodged another rocket. Cavallos swung the M-60 at the target. The two men below were reloading for a third shot. Cavallos pulled the trigger, and flame flashed from the muzzle. Their bodies dropped in a heap, with the RPG and extra rocket rolling away. Cavallos grabbed the loose headset and told Roxana to go back.

Bullets from al-Bazr's handgun nicked the chopper. The Rover's driver stood through the sunroof firing his pistol.

The M-60 hammered some more. Cavallos cut the Rover nearly in half, the driver's upper body exploding with hits. The last burst from the M-60 cut down al-Bazr, slicing his legs out from under him.

Roxana set down and handed Cavallos her pistol. Cavallos jumped out and ran toward al-Bazr, who screamed at the sky, his wrecked legs mocking his attempts to move. His blood turned the grass and dirt under him into a red muck. He stopped screaming when he saw Cavallos.

Cavallos raised the pistol and shot al-Bazr in the head. The man jerked as the bullet plowed through, and then his body lay still. Cavallos picked up the briefcase, opened it to be sure and tossed it away. The case had only been weighted with books. He spat on al-Bazr's body.

Back in the chopper, he let out a breath as Roxana lifted off again.

"After all that," she said, "we only have enough fuel to get halfway to where we left the car."

"Then we'll have a nice hike," he said, adding, "This didn't happen to those other fellows."

Presently they landed, rigging a charge to blow up the chopper, and spent two hours hiking to where they had a car stashed. From there it took another hour to reach the motorway, and less than twenty-four hours later Cavallos and his wife reached London, where they parked beneath a hotel where they earlier had reserved a room.

They'd spent a ton of money and now had bupkis to show for the effort. They did not discuss or argue about the situation, but instead took turns in the shower and then had meals sent up before going to sleep.

"Tomorrow will be better," Roxana said as she rolled over and dozed off.

But Cavallos lay on his back staring at the ceiling. Al-Qaeda would not sit still after what had happened. The order would go out for their assassination. Perhaps a reward would be posted, and freelance hitters would make a play. Running from the Western police and intelligence forces was one thing; al-Qaeda was another story.

And they had no sanctuary. Cavallos let out a sigh and lay awake for a long time.

Cavallos didn't awaken the next morning until he smelled bacon. He raised his head to see Roxana setting plates on the table. Bacon, scrambled eggs, hash browns and coffee.

"You slept like a log," she said.

"Felt like I was awake most of the night."

He brushed his teeth and joined her at the table.

"That was good flying yesterday," he said between bites.

She smiled and poured sugar into her coffee. The smile faded and her eyes told him something else.

"We'll be okay," he said.

"You always say that."

"Have I ever been wrong?"

"When we were young—"

"Please, Roxana. Let's not dwell on our decisions. We can always give up and spend the rest of our lives in prison."

"You'll spend them alone. I'll die first."

"Then we wait for something to turn up. It will."

They ate quietly for a while.

"How about Paris for a few days?"

Cavallos nodded. "We could..." and he stopped talking at the sight of a black car pulling up across the street. Four men exited.

Special Branch?

No. The four men had darker skin than the average Briton.

"They're here," Cavallos said, and bolted from the table.

Roxana, already dressed, grabbed their tote bags and car keys. Cavallos jumped into yesterday's clothes and zipped a jacket over the pistol his wife gave him.

"We can't have a fight here," she said.

He nodded and they left the room, skipping the elevator for the stairwell. As the stairwell door closed behind them, the elevator dinged open and the four men from the car emerged. They drew pistols and advanced toward the empty room.

Chapter Fourteen

Theodore Stanton Trent had nothing to do.

The technicians at the test site were doing all the work, monitoring equipment in the bunker, preparing the target that sat down range. He stood in the back, almost in the corner, a naughty child facing forward during a time-out.

The narrow stone bunker, built eight feet into the earth, really didn't have the extra space for him. Rows of computer monitors lined the front. Servers and other electrical components took up the rest of the wall space. Techs sat elbow to elbow in front of their workstations. Other techs squeezed by Trent as they went out to check the target.

The target down range was a World War Two–vintage tank, an M3 Light Tank. The techs, a humorous sort, had painted a yellow smiley face on the side. Trent hated to destroy the old relic but took solace in that it was once again serving its country.

Trent stood well over six feet, a little soft in the middle from so many years spent behind a drafting table and far too many good dinners to discuss business, but he was otherwise fit, with sharp blue eyes and most of his hair, which had prematurely turned gray in his 30s. He'd let the gray remain because it added character and showed he was a man of experience.

"M-113 on the way," one of the techs said. Trent stepped outside to watch the arrival.

The bunker and testing area occupied a small portion of the 200 acres of country behind Trent Defense. The sprawling complex, located in southern Texas near Corpus Christi, had been his base of operations for nearly twenty years.

The M-113, a track-and-wheel armored transport with a cannon on the roof, rumbled toward the bunker. It followed well-worn tracks in the dirt. It wasn't a standard M-113. A parabolic dish was mounted on the roof, behind the cannon, connected to electrical equipment in the back cargo area. The M-113 stopped next to the bunker. The engine grumbled. The hydraulic brakes hissed. Two technicians hopped out, and one made adjustments in the back while the other climbed a ladder to the dish. The tech manually positioned the dish so it pointed at the M3 tank. Trent watched without comment. Today's test wasn't to see if what he'd worked so hard to build would work. He knew it worked from previous tests. Today's effort was to make sure there were no kinks prior to demonstrating the weapon for the Russians.

He'd named it the M-680c, the "c" designation meaning it was the third version.

Trent felt a little sad watching them work. There was a time when he would have been one of those boys, fiddling and tinkering and fixing and building; now, he pushed paper and raised money while the real engineers played in his sandbox.

But that was life. That was progress. Because what the engineers were working on was a long-held vision finally coming to life.

Trent had dreamed of creating a laser gun, the official phrase being the less cool "direct energy weapon," back in his 20s when sitting in a theater watching *Star Wars* for the umpteenth time in 1977. The ability to harness direct energy, and channel it at a specific target, had taken decades to go from theoretical to practical.

The techs at the M-113 announced all was ready. One hopped back in the cabin to sit behind the firing controls. A monitor showed a bull's-eye on the tank; a joystick with a trigger would fire the weapon when the time came.

"T minus five," the lead tech in the cabin announced.

The tech in the firing seat flipped switches, and the dish started to hum. Trent returned to the bunker. The monitors showed a red dot landing on the yellow smiley face as well as other technical information that updated so fast, Trent couldn't keep up.

The tech at the firing seat wrapped a hand around the joystick and pulled the trigger. The M-680c took forty-five seconds to fire, and when the pulse activated, there was no sound or any indication from the dish. The tank just exploded. The flash filled the monitors, and the ground shook. If you didn't know the dish had fired, it looked as if the tank had spontaneously combusted. Pieces of the tank rained down over a black spot on the dirt where the tank once sat. None of the debris landed on the bunker.

"Excellent," Trent said. He laughed a little, unable to contain the joy of watching his life's work take final form. "Is there anything else we can blow up?"

Trent returned to his office, which was on the first floor of the main building, rear parking lot and part of the cityscape beyond visible from his window. He could have taken an office on the upper floor, as any other company president indeed did, but after forty years of working, he refused to ride an elevator or take stairs in his own building.

He sat at his desk, bifocals at the edge of his nose, typing notes into a computer document. He worked in a large office, black tiled floor with gray walls, paintings here and there, no bookcases. He did have a small fridge in the corner for sodas and his lunch, along with the usual desktop computer and printer adjoining the desk.

Having worked his way through college with a company that sold oil and gas to the army, he had made plenty of defense industry contacts that were eager to bring him aboard once he'd earned his degree in mechanical engineering. Further education in applied physics came when the idea for a laser weapon dug into his head, yet at the time he lacked the knowledge to make the idea a reality. He was one of many exploring such dreams. Not getting the US contract to build deployable direct energy weapons wasn't the result of inferior tech, but of the usual shenanigans that befell any federal contract. Not enough palms greased, or not the lowest bid.

The loss hurt, nonetheless.

Enter the Russians. Would they like a demonstration of a fantastic new weapon? Yes, indeed.

Trent was old enough, unlike most of his current engineering staff, to remember Russia as the enemy.

Now they were a potential new revenue source. It amazed him how the world had changed in such a short time.

Trent finished typing as his office door opened and a young woman entered. Dark skirt, blouse, high heels tapping on the tiled floor. She wore her hair in a ponytail, and the tail bounced as she moved. Her brown eyes matched her late mother's—Colleen Trent was her father's daughter, however.

"Hi." She sat in front of his desk and crossed her legs. Colleen was an engineer, too, and worked in research and development.

"Just got your notes finished," Trent said. The printer hummed to life and spit out two pages, which Trent collected and handed to his daughter. She gave him a look as he sat down, and he shifted uncomfortably under the stare.

"What is it?"

"I don't agree with your trip to Monaco or this Russian deal."

"Colleen—"

"Are you even watching what's happening in the world?"

"They aren't the enemy anymore, Colleen. They're nothing like when I was *your* age and nuclear war was a distinct possibility. Times change."

"Putin sends out his bombers to violate NATO and US airspace like it's some sort of game. It's classic saber rattling, Dad. If you sell to him—"

"Honey, stop. We've worked too long and hard not to sell our product."

"A *product*, as you say, that in the wrong hands gives the world another way to destroy itself."

"Do I have to remind you of all the money we've spent? We can't just write it off. We'll go bankrupt."

"Have you thought about retooling for medical purposes?"

Trent let out a breath.

"I've been doing the prelim," she said, "and put together a presentation on how, with just a little more time and investment, we could actually revolutionize the use of lasers in medicine and help people instead of blowing them up."

"How much time and investment?"

"Five years and less than ten million."

"That's a little more than what you have in your purse, I assume."

"What?"

"We don't have the money, Colleen. It all went into the 680 to win a contract we lost. We have to at least meet with the Russians. I can't cancel."

"Maybe they won't buy, either."

"Maybe," he said.

"Then what, we're on the street?"

"There will be severe cuts."

Colleen's shoulders sank a little. "At least watch my presentation on the plane." She handed him a pink thumb drive from her jacket pocket.

Trent took it. "Those notes tell what I need done while I'm gone and I want you to take care of it."

"Fine." She rose stiffly, and her heels clicked again on her way out the door.

Trent turned the pink thumb drive over in his fingers. He'd do what she'd asked, of course, no question, but if she knew just how close to the precipice the company was, she'd understand more why he was being so stubborn. To tell her too much, though, would worry her. He didn't want that. She had enough on her mind, and he knew she still heavily felt the loss of her mother.

It was why she was working for him. She didn't want to be too far away in case she lost him, too.

What she didn't know wouldn't keep her up at night. Trent was old enough to miss a few hours of sleep now and then.

Chapter Fifteen

Steve Dane reduced the speed of the treadmill and began a cool-down after logging five miles. Sweat coated his upper body and made his shirt cling to his skin. He was the only one in the hotel gym wearing a long-sleeved button-down shirt with his running shorts. He looked silly, but he didn't want the puckered, fire-scarred flesh on his right side and arm exposed for everyone to see. Maybe that was sillier. The scars reminded him that he wasn't invincible. He didn't need that thought haunting the back of his mind. He saw the scars enough already. The thoughts were also never far from him anyway. It was all for naught. But he'd never admit that.

A helicopter crash had almost killed him, but he'd escaped with the burns, back when he was a CIA agent. His partner, Len Lukavina, had been with him at the time. Len hadn't been as lucky. He couldn't hide his scars, since part of his face had caught fire.

The crash had been a freak accident, sure. Typical Murphy's Law. It was an event extreme enough to leave an impression Dane would never forget. Every day was a gift, his life to be lived at full speed, and on his own terms.

He slowed the treadmill more as a blonde man entered the gym and started on the bench press: John Blaze, Nina's thief. He only seemed like another tourist, and Dane wondered if they were watching him for no reason. The activity kept Nina from being B-O-R-E-D, and, more important, kept her happy, and when Nina was happy, Dane wasn't miserable. She had to keep a low profile, however. If she recognized him, he might recognize her. He'd certainly spot a surveillance routine. As long as they knew his general area of movement, they didn't watch too closely.

Dane slowed the treadmill to walking speed and hopped off. He dried his face.

Blaze, at the bench press, lifted steadily, breathing in and out with each lift, but he had no spotter. Dane wandered over.

"Need a spot?"

"Thanks, mate. Going a little heavier today. Gotta burn off last night's dessert."

"Don't I know it."

Blaze slowed as he went over ten reps, his face showing the strain. At twenty his face took on a reddish tinge. He pressed the barbell up with more effort than before, and Dane grabbed the bar and helped Blaze put it back on the rack.

"Thanks," Blaze said, breathing hard. He lay on the bench a little longer, then Dane helped him up.

"New record," the thief said. "You here by yourself?"

"On holiday with my lady friend."

"Plenty of ladies here if you ever come alone," Blaze said. "I'm riding solo. Waiting for some work to come along. May have to leave quickly."

"What do you do?"

"Freelance search and recovery. If something gets lost, I go find it."

Dane smiled. *The lies we tell.* "Have fun," he said. "I gotta meet the lady for lunch."

"Thanks for the spot," Blaze said as he moved to a treadmill.

With his towel over his shoulder, Dane returned to his room. A note from Nina, stuck on the television, simply said: *Gone shopping.* In other words, spending more of his money. Or was it *their* money? They certainly earned enough together that he should probably cut her some slack in the accounting department, but most of their operating funds came from his captured South African diamond cache, money *he* had secured.

But they were a team, so maybe he needed to adjust his attitude. They could always find more money somewhere. Start charging potential clients, the ones who could afford a large free, instead of always working *gratis.*

After showering, he dressed in a blue shirt with black slacks, and decided his shoes needed a shine. He went downstairs. He sat in the hotel barber shop while an old Italian shined the shoes mirror bright and Dane gave him a large tip. Then he searched the hotel's mini-mall looking for Nina. He found her in the third shop he tried. She was looking at summer dresses, flicking through them in quick succession with growing irritation.

"You're not carrying any bags," he noted.

Nina continued sorting angrily. "Can't find my size," she said. "Apparently I'm not skinny enough."

"Skinny girls run the world."

"There should be a violent coup that ends at a guillotine."

With a gasp of victory, she finally selected a flower print. "I'll be right back."

"What's the price?"

"Go to hell."

Dane laughed as she marched into a fitting room and shut the door. He went over and knocked.

"Need any help?"

"What did I just say?"

He found a nearby padded bench and sat to dumbly observe other shoppers, all young women, who ignored him. He wanted to talk to the proprietor and inquire about installing a television or a bar for the men who had to wait while their women shopped. It was a potential revenue source, for sure, and a great place to meet women if a fellow was on the prowl.

Dane then decided if saving the world didn't work out, he might start a consulting business, help others get rich, and really make a killing. Write a book, go on speaking tours, the ideas were endless.

Maybe he was getting a little B-O-R-E-D too.

Presently she stepped out and modeled the outfit. Dane raised an eyebrow. It didn't fit her figure at all, too side at the hips, and the straps over her shoulders were working hard not to lose coverage in front. They were losing the fight.

"What do you think?" She posed in front of a wall-mounted mirror.

Dane raised an eyebrow. "Looks lovely." There was no delight in his voice. He hoped Nina saw what he saw.

"It is awful," she stated. "I look like a potato sack. With boobs."

That was close. "Well…"

"Quiet!"

She went back to the fitting room. Dane let out a breath. The dress had not fit well indeed. Nina emerged in her other clothes. She returned the dress to the rack, and they left the shop hand in hand before discovering a brightly lit seafood restaurant free of gaudy plastic fish decorations on the walls—a surprise to Dane. The hostess sat them in a booth.

He told her about his chat with John Blaze.

"Is he waiting for something here," Nina said, "or will he go someplace else?"

"Who knows? I think we should stop watching him and see if any VIPs show up."

"This place is full of VIPs."

"And yet he's made no moves," Dane said. "For somebody who targets the rich, he's ignoring a lot of potential targets. He might be waiting for somebody specific."

"There is a reward out for his capture, by the way," Nina said. "I made some calls after you left for the gym. The Moscow police are offering five thousand, US, but De Beers is offering two million."

"Why?"

"He allegedly stole five uncut diamonds from one of their couriers."

Dane nodded. The diamond syndicate didn't mess around when it came to diamonds in any shape or form, and especially when the diamonds in question were their property. They'd tried to muscle in on his South Africa arrangement, but he'd deterred their efforts with the snout of his .45. If their split offer had been better, he might have taken the deal, but they'd wanted too much of the boodle.

Chapter Sixteen

The waiter arrived to take their orders. Fish and chips for Dane, grilled salmon and salad for Nina.

"You keep eating fried food," she said, "and your stomach will revolt again."

"I feel fine now. And I hardly *ever* eat fried stuff."

"Don't say I didn't warn you."

When the waiter departed, Nina said, "Let's hit Blaze over the head and take him to De Beers. I won't get out of bed for Moscow's money."

"You're talking out of your butt, dear."

"Am I?"

"You want to know what he's up to as much as I do. You think there's a bigger prize, same as I do. We aren't going to find out what that is if we take him in like a couple of bounty hunters."

"Bounty hunting isn't so bad," Nina said.

"Really?"

"They get their own television shows. We'd be good on television, don't you think?"

"I want to have a cable show," Dane said. "Then we

won't have to censor the bad language or the sex scenes."

Nina scoffed. "Forget that. The camera adds ten pounds."

Dane ate a piece of fish. "Eat up, dear. I'm working on my ten right now." He grinned at her.

She kicked him under the table. He stifled a grunt.

Theodore Stanton Trent crossed the Hotel de Monte Carlo's lobby. He was so focused that he didn't take in the ornate architecture and went straight to the check-in desk. While a young man processed his credit card, he said, "Has a guest named Alexander Arkady arrived?"

"I'm afraid I can't say, sir," the man said, passing Trent a form. Trent filled in the blank lines. The young man returned his credit card along with a room key and wished him an enjoyable stay.

Trent grumbled about hotel discretion but decided he wouldn't want anybody to simply ask about his room, either. He was nervous. He'd only had one cup of coffee before his flight, but he still felt jittery, as if he'd had too much. He needed to relax. There was a lot riding on the deal, but if he didn't settle down, he'd blow the opportunity. Nobody liked working with a man who appeared desperate.

He found the elevators and pressed the button for the twenty-first floor, noting that even in Monaco, they did not include a thirteenth floor.

He traveled alone, no entourage. He'd closed a ton of deals on his own throughout his career and he didn't need anybody else's objection. Colleen's words still weighed on his mind and she couldn't have been the only one to hold thoughts of opposition. She was, however, the only one willing to voice them.

She normally had zero reservations about their work and had contributed to the M-680 project as much as anybody. She had to feel very strongly specifically about this meeting to try to change his mind. He loved her for it, but she wasn't the only person he had to think about. His company was at stake, as well as the livelihoods of every single employee and supplier. They had all put in too much to go unrewarded.

He had selfish reasons, too. He didn't want to leave behind a legacy of failure. To close up shop meant exactly that. He'd worked too hard, for too long, to not reach the finish line.

He had to admit, however, as he entered his room and placed his bags on the bed, that her alternative plan looked very attractive.

He filled the dresser drawers with clothes and hung an extra suit in the closet. He did not open the curtains to see the outside view. Instead he spread on the writing table the partial blueprint of the M-680c and photos of various tests. He had videos of the tests on his laptop. He hoped they were enough to get the interest of the Russians.

He sat and examined the documents, going over in his head what he'd say at the meeting, with a nagging thought about Colleen's presentation piggybacking on his strategy. He knew nothing about the medical field. All he'd ever made was military equipment. They might be able to transition, but the cost of failure outweighed the financial commitment.

The Russian deal had to go through.

Marco Cavallos thanked the waitress for the espresso and sipped the hot drink.

He and Roxana had traveled as far as Siena, Italy, where

they'd been hiding out for the past twenty-four hours.

When Alexander Arkady had called to ask for a meeting, they heartily agreed. They needed to replenish what they'd spent on the botched prison rescue. The Russians paid well, and on time. It was the kind of deal they needed badly. But Cavallos had more on his mind than money. Another form of compensation might come from the hands of the Kremlin if he asked nicely.

He sat alone in the back of a small café, near the kitchen, where cooking sounds and shouts in Italian drowned out the quiet music filling the rest of the space.

Roxana sat in the outside sitting area, pistol and car keys at the ready, in case they needed to get away fast. They had parked the car near the alley behind the café.

The hawk-faced Russian, in a black suit and coat, entered and Cavallos waved him over. The Russian ordered black coffee.

"You're alone?" Arkady said.

"No. What's going on?"

"We have a job for you in the United States," Arkady said. "I need an expert at industrial removal."

Cavallos nodded. The espresso had cooled, and he drank a little.

"Twenty million US," the Russian said.

Cavallos let out a low whistle. "That's fine, but we need more than money this time."

"Hmmm?"

"Last job went bad. We're on the run."

"You're always on the run, Marco."

"Al-Qaeda this time."

Arkady drank some coffee. "So?"

"Ten million US and sanctuary in Russia."

"Sanctuary?"

"A home base for us."

"I don't know—"

"Five million."

"You're desperate," Arkady said.

"We can't run forever."

"Okay. Ten million and we let you into Russia. You're responsible for a domicile. There will be no guarantee of protection if you are caught on Russian soil."

"Not a problem."

"And you'll be on call for us. Gratis."

"You expect a need?"

"We'll create a need if we must. That's the deal. Take it or leave it."

"We'll take it."

"You don't need to speak with your wife?"

"Don't worry about her. When do you need us in America?"

"A few days. Texas, specifically. First, I need you in Monaco. Brief side trip, won't take long."

"Wire the payment to the usual account."

"Half now."

"Of course."

Arkady finished his coffee. "Hotel de Monte Carlo by tomorrow morning."

"We'll be there."

"I'll find you."

"You'll be there?"

"Yes."

The Russian left the table. Cavallos settled the bill, wondering what the Hawk had in mind. He exited onto the sidewalk and flashed a hand signal to his wife. She joined him in the car a few minutes later, and he told her about the deal.

"Russia gets so cold in the winter," she said.

"I don't see another option."

She squeezed his hand. "We'll find a way to stay warm."

He started the car.

Chapter Seventeen

Dane and Nina sat in another booth in yet another of the hotel's restaurants, a steakhouse this time with low light. A candle flickered in the center of their table.

"Maybe I can seduce him," Nina said.

Dane sipped his martini. "Won't work," he said.

Blaze sat alone at another table across the dining room. He had not seen Dane upon entering.

"Why not?"

"You'll spend all your time thinking of me."

"You're right. And he'll wonder why I'm lying there like a dead fish while he's on top grunting and sweating."

Dane smiled, eyes on Blaze.

"Maybe *you* should seduce him," Nina said. "He's British, you know."

"What does that mean?"

"The Brits invented homosexuality. Ever hear the joke about the Prime Minister's assistant who woke him early in the morning to say the Defense Minister had been caught in a bed with somebody not his wife? The PM said, 'Please tell me is was a woman!'"

Dane chuckled. "That's enough."

She swallowed a slug of vodka and sat with her back to Blaze. "What's he doing now?"

"He's taking an interest in a new arrival."

A tall man with thin gray hair and glasses. The hostess showed him to a table.

Nina turned to look. "Who is he?"

"Could be the target. Blaze hasn't looked at anybody else except the waitresses."

"How do we find out who this person is?"

The waiter brought dinner. Dane told Nina halfway through the meal that he had an idea. After he paid the check, Dane brought Nina to the center of the restaurant where a fountain sat, the quiet waterfall taking the place of mood music. Dane used her iPhone and made sure the tall man was in the picture while she posed near the fountain.

Back in their room, Dane and Nina sat at the writing table, where Nina cropped herself out of the photo and tapped the screen a few more times to email the picture to Todd McConn.

Dane then used his own phone to call McConn, who answered on the third ring. "What's today's problem?" McConn said.

"I just sent you a picture," Dane said.

Nina called out, "I sent the picture!"

"I need an ID and whatever else you can get."

"Got it. Give me a half hour."

Nina poured a glass of Bereau for herself and a Jack and Coke for Dane. They sat out on the patio and looked to the horizon, where the ocean met the night sky. A light breeze ruffled Nina's skirt. Dane lit a H. Upmann 1844 Reserve and blew smoke at the stars.

"What if the tall man is worth stealing from?" Nina

said, and sipped her wine. It was one of the most expensive French reds available. Seventy-six hundred bucks a case. She hadn't told Dane the cost.

"What do you mean?"

"What if he's a gangster or some other no-goodnik who deserves a licking?"

"We'll know soon, but what are you getting at?"

"It might be worthwhile to help Blaze get away and catch him later," she said.

"Let the ungodly suffer, you mean."

"If we stop Blaze, we might prevent something that shouldn't be prevented. It's just a suggestion."

"Drink your vitamins, dear."

She sipped her wine and laughed, her laughter sounding like tinkling wind chimes. The sound made Dane feel good.

McConn called back an hour later.

"Took longer than I thought. You found a good one."

"Let's hear it," Dane said. He put McConn on speaker and they both listened.

"Theodore Trent, sixty-four, president of Trent Defense. Major player in defense industry. He's upset some people at the State Department."

"Why?"

"He's in Monaco to meet with a Russian representative to talk about a direct energy weapon. Ever hear of that?"

"Just enough," Dane said, "to know I don't like them."

Nina said, "Is it a popcorn maker?"

"Trent lost a government contract to build DEWs for the army," McConn continued, "so he's offering the tech to Russia. Could be a billion-dollar deal over time."

"Well he's here, so State didn't stop him."

"He's not breaking any laws. Russia isn't the bad guy anymore."

"Give them time."

Nina punched Dane in the arm. He winced but ignored her.

"That's all I got," McConn said.

"It'll do for a start. Thanks, Todd."

Dane ended the call and put the phone down.

Nina said, "It's not a popcorn maker?"

Dane exhaled a cloud of smoke. "Those damn eggheads never stop."

"Trent has made a laser gun?"

"Or something close. If he's meeting somebody here, he has material related to the weapon that Blaze probably wants. Blaze might have been sent by the US. He might be working for a third party." He cursed and puffed on his cigar. "Why do we need laser weapons? It's not as if the human race can't destroy itself ten times over with what we already have. The US has lasers so now the Russians want them and maybe another country, too, because the Sheldon Coopers of the world simply *must* make *Star Trek* real so they can live out juvenile comic book fantasies because women won't touch them. It's insanity."

"Human nature," Nina said. "We do things because we can. We flew to the moon because it was there."

"*Americans* flew to the moon," Dane said, "to beat *your* people there. To prove the Nazi scientists who built our rockets were better than the Nazi scientists who built your rockets. It was about winning the Cold War. Peace for All Mankind was a cute slogan."

"Before our time, honey."

"There's always another agenda. Nobody does anything with pure motives. Least of all any government."

"What do we do now?"

"I'd very much like to collect two million dollars from De Beers," Dane said, "and take whatever documents Blaze plans steals from Trent."

"That won't stop anything. Trent has only brought copies of work that's safe and secure in the United States."

"It might make it more complicated for somebody," Dane said. "We take what little victories we can get."

Chapter Eighteen

Alexander Arkady arrived the next afternoon and unpacked his bags. He opened the hotel room window to let in the sea air and took a deep breath. Moscow may have been home, but even somebody as patriotic as he had to admit the world offered many glorious places to visit, and that the blue sky and ocean before him sure beat the overcast drabness of Moscow.

He left the window open to let the air circulate through the room while he went to the casino. He was not good at table games of any kind, but he did enjoy slot machines, and played a succession of them to break almost even. The newer video machines were not as fun as the mechanical one-armed bandits he remembered from his youth, but they helped pass the time, nonetheless.

He stood and watched a busy craps game, staying well back from the fray and clinking the coins in his hands. A young woman was throwing the dice and having a grand old time as others at the table bet on her outcomes. Words like "hot table" and "let it ride" and "hard eight" came his way, but Arkady didn't understand the lingo.

"Some game," said a man who came up beside the Hawk.

Arkady turned. The man beside him was Cavallos. The two men did not shake hands or smile. Their faces remained stoic.

"Keep an eye on room 2112," the Russian said. "Surveillance only." Arkady passed Cavallos a duplicate key card to Trent's room. "Compliments of our technical section. It will open any room in the building."

"We can loot the place and make some extra money."

Arkady did not laugh. "No."

Cavallos took the key and melted back into the casino traffic.

Arkady returned to the slots. The brightly lighted machines were of great interest. They all offered the same thing, a chance to win money depending upon which combination of numbers or symbols turned up on the digital display. But game designers did not simply make one machine and leave it at that. A variety of machines, with colorful graphics, some boasting titles of Western movies and television shows, and containing associated artwork, waited for dedicated slots players. Arkaday moved through the sea of people and machines looking for the right one to sit at. He couldn't help but notice those already seated looked like robots. They stared blankly at the spinning displays, pressing buttons or pulling levers, smoking, drinking, killing time. Gambling their lives away for a fortune forever out of reach.

The slot players were a metaphor for the West and all of its indignities. If the energy of the people were directed, by a benevolent government, into proper activities, they would find a greater purpose in life than sitting in front of a machine hoping a jackpot might fall into their ample laps.

Someday. Someday they will be shown the truth.

The slot machines all offered the same type of game, but the way people moved from one machine to the next, the variety of designs at least held an appeal. Either that, or they felt some machines "more lucky" than others. Arkady didn't agree with that. If you're losing a battle, you can't move to another. You have to stay on the front until you're either defeated or the turn the tide with superior firepower or superior forces. Either way, patience was the key.

And the Hawk had perfected patience during his years of service to the Motherland.

Regarding Cavallos and his wife, Putin had, without argument, granted permission for the couple to relocate to Russia at the close of their assignment. Perhaps he'd been more pleased at not having to pay the full twenty million, or he liked the idea of the pair's being at his beck and call. As long as they completed their mission, they could peacefully settle in the Motherland for the foreseeable future. Neither al-Qaeda nor anybody else would dare to move against them on Russian soil.

Arkady found a corner slot machine displaying American and European sports cars as its motif. He knew a little about sports cars, but the vehicles held no real interest. He inserted money into a slot and pressed the bet button and then the spin button. The symbols on the screen, cars and numbers and shapes, spun quickly, the machine emitted an engine noise. A horn honked when the display stopped. A loss. Arkady pressed Repeat Bet. Engine, honk. He laughed. Without realizing, he, too, became transfixed by the spinning display, the rising and falling total, and kept hitting Repeat Bet until his money was exhausted. He rose from the chair with a smile. Easy come, easy go. There was always more money somewhere. And he'd enjoyed the two hours he'd sat letting his mind detach from current issues.

Maybe he shouldn't be so hard on the "robots" around him. Perhaps they knew something he didn't.

He checked his watch. He and Trent had scheduled their preliminary getting-to-know-you dinner for that evening. His two hours at the slot machine brought him within ten minutes of the scheduled time. The Texan might be a bore but Arkady would still go through the motions. If he had to pull a takeaway to make Trent nervous, he'd have to know when to start and, more important, when to stop. It was a lot to go through for just a performance, but he needed Trent to lower his defenses.

John Blaze sat in a bar staring into his Scotch. Tonight was finally the night for action. He'd watched Trent the evening before but found no opportunity to make a move. Now both Trent and Arkady were present and accounted for, and he had his action plan. A prefabricated door card that would spoof any lock waited in his wallet. If hotels around the world realized how easy it was to duplicate key cards, they'd find another way to keep rooms secured. All one needed was a chip programmed with enough frequencies to match the receiver in the doors. It might take a minute, but eventually the signals would mesh and the locks click back.

The past couple of days had offered little joy because of his foreboding about the job. He was a good thief, yes. He'd escaped many a police manhunt. But the butterflies in his belly prior to every job had to be dealt with via a series of mental exercises to "pump up" his "thieving muscles". The exercises included visualizing the job, every step, along with possible complications that might arise and options for dealing with those issues. Tonight, doubts were gone. He was ready. Now he could get to work, and then slip away to find another place to unwind, perhaps find another Countess Fromme to impress.

He finished his drink and left the bar, making the rounds of the restaurants on the pretext of looking for a friend. The restaurants were open in front, facing the walkway off the casino floor, with walls blocking off the dining room from the kitchen. It was easy to scan the tables. Helpful hostesses offered to assist but he politely declined. When he spotted Trent and Arkady dining at the steakhouse with no documents present at the table, he knew the perfect time to strike had arrived.

His shoes tapped on marble tile as he headed for the elevators. He cut through a swath of well-dressed men and women who were part of a large group and having a very good time, most glassy-eyed, only one or two sharp enough to communicate that they were the sober ones of the party.

Stepping into an elevator with a trio of tipsy women laughing about a private joke, he made his way to the twenty-first floor. He exited, leaving the women behind, and their laugher faded as the doors slid shut behind Blaze. The hallway was quiet but for the hum of the HVAC system.

In front of the elevator was a small sitting area.

A woman, alone, occupied a seat, reading a magazine. She had short hair with blonde highlights and wore a blue cocktail dress that fit tightly over her svelte curves. She paid him no attention. The wedding ring on her left hand contained a diamond bigger than the Rock of Gibraltar. Blaze smiled. Was she like the Countess? Could he add that rock to his collection?

Fun later. Work now.

Blaze turned his eyes away and turned right and walked down the hall. He took out his wallet and removed the copied door card. When he reached Trent's room, he slipped the card into the lock and waited. Presently the red light on the door unit turned green and the lock clicked. Blaze entered the dark room and shut the door behind him, throwing the secondary hook lock as an extra hedge of defense against Trent's sudden return.

A pocket pen flash led the way to the room's electronic safe, which sat on the carpet near the dresser, bolted to the floor and the wall. *Almost as easy to pick as the door*, Blaze thought, grinning as he got to work. The butterflies had been replaced by a sense of determination, that of a shark pursuing quarry at full speed.

From under his jacket, Blaze removed a rectangular leather case about six inches long. He unzipped the case and removed a plastic rod with a wire at one end that had a small connector at the end that would fit into the recharging slot of his iPhone. Next, Blaze took out the phone and plugged the wire into the slot. The phone screen lit up. He removed a side panel near the top of the safe with a small screwdriver, also taken from the leather case. He slid the plastic rod into a hole, stopping halfway. The phone screen showed a series of numbers cycling like one of the slot machines in the casino. Blaze left the phone, went into the bathroom and splashed some water on his face. No matter how many jobs he pulled, no matter how he pushed the butterflies away, he always ended up soaked with sweat. He already felt his shirt sticking to his torso. Now was no different. He wiped his face on a towel and tossed it on the counter. Blaze returned to the safe. One number on the readout had stopped at five. Three more numbers to go.

Chapter Nineteen

The woman in the hallway sitting area, Roxana Cavallos, set down the magazine and reached for the diamond-studded purse on the seat beside her. Unlocking the jeweled clasp, she took out her cell and called her husband.

"Somebody not Trent is in Trent's room."

"Be right up."

Roxana replaced the phone in her purse, wedging it next to a silenced Kimber Ultra Covert .45 ACP. The suppressor made the pistol forward-heavy, requiring her to cock her wrist to properly align the muzzle with a target, but the subsonic .45 ammo worked well under suppression and the brass of an ejected cartridge bouncing off the hotel room wall would make more noise than the shot.

All she had to do right now was wait for her husband.

Blaze wiped his face with a towel and took deep breaths as the numbers on the iPhone screen continued to cycle. The second number, four, solidified; two remained.

He wiped sweat from his forehead. There was still a lot that could go wrong. If his device suddenly failed before cracking the safe's code, he was sunk. If somebody came through the door, he had no reason for being there, and that meant somebody might get shot. He was armed, albeit with a small pistol, and he knew how to use the weapon should the need arise.

He'd never killed anybody in the course of an assignment. The Trust didn't use him as an assassin.

But the moment might arrive where he needed to choose between his life and somebody else's.

He hoped it wasn't tonight.

Roxana tapped her feet with eyes fixed down the length of the hallway. The camera in the upper corner above the elevators meant that overt action against the intruder when he reappeared was out of the question. If Marco didn't get here, she'd have to let him go, and that could wreck the whole job.

Failing to stop Blaze would do more than wreck the whole job. The failure would jeopardize their agreement with the Russians. Her heartrate increased. That couldn't happen. If she had to go alone, Blaze wasn't walking out of that room alive.

The elevator dinged and the doors slid open. Marco Cavallos stepped out and said, "Let's go."

Roxana rose from the chair with a huge sense of relief. The two of them advanced down the hall.

Roxana took out her Kimber as Cavallos removed the duplicate key card handed to him earlier by Arkady. They reached 2112. No light spilled from under the door. Cavallos slipped the card into the slot. The lock clicked. Cavallos pushed the door open but it jammed, caught on the secondary hook.

"Back," Roxana said. Cavallos complied. Roxana

raised her pistol and fired. The shots sounded like a loud thud. The doorframe splintered at the base of the hook and she shoved open the door, the Kimber .45 leading the way. Cavallos followed with his own silenced Browning 9mm in his right hand.

The numbers on the display showed three with one to go.

Blaze wiped his face again.

Not much longer. He took a deep breath and willed the software to go faster.

The door lock clicked. It started to swing open, stopping solidly on the secondary hook. Blaze jumped back from the safe, drawing a .25 Beretta from under his jacket. A silenced shot shattered the doorframe, breaking the hook loose, and the door swung inward.

The light of the hallway outlined the two new arrivals, and Blaze recognized the woman as the one he'd passed in the hall. She braced against the wall and leveled the snout of a suppressor-fitted .45, but he fired first. The little .25 popped twice. The woman screamed and recoiled back, her male counterpart stepping in front of her. Blaze tightened his trigger finger again but the automatic in the other man's hand thumped first. The first round tore through Blaze's chest. The second snapped back his head. He collapsed onto the carpet.

Cavallos knelt beside his wife. He was calm on the outside, but his pulse raced inside. The hit hadn't gone as planned. They were supposed to shoot and scoot. Now he had a wounded wife to take care of. He examined her. Normally taking in every inch of her toned body was a pleasure, but not this time. He was looking for holes that shouldn't be there, blood on the dress, indications that she needed immediate medical help. But her dress was clean. A little out of shape from the way she fell, but not blood stained at all. She pushed up from the floor with a wince.

"I'm fine," she said.

"How?"

"He missed." She pointed at the wall where she had positioned her. Both .25 slugs had gouged the sheetrock, unable to penetrate through. She picked out one slug with her fingernails and tossed it to Cavallos, who pocketed it.

"I was startled by how close he got, though," she said.

"Hmmm."

The iPhone plugged into the floor safe beeped. Cavallos punched the four numbers into the keypad and wrenched open the door. He took the items inside, mostly papers and a laptop. The laptop rode in a carrying case, and Cavallos jammed the papers inside the case as well. He threw the case over his shoulder.

Cavallos and his wife left the room, using the stairwell, which didn't have the camera coverage that the elevators had. They entered their floor and Cavallos led his wife back to their room.

In the bathroom she splashed water on her face. Cavallos watched her pull off the party dress and throw her arms through a bathrobe. The party dress remained a sparkly pile on the floor. As she tied it around her waist, she said, "I need a shower after that."

"Right. I'll go see Trent."

"Hey."

"What?"

"Whatever is in that bag, the Russians obviously want it badly."

"So?"

"Maybe we should try selling it back to them."

"We honor the deal we made," Cavallos said. "We have enough people looking for us. I'm not adding the Russians to the list. They'll succeed where everybody else failed."

"I guess."

"Take your shower," Cavallos said. He left the room.

Chapter Twenty

The quiet trickle of water from the steakhouse fountain couldn't overcome the buzz of conversation.

Trent waited nervously at the table, a glass of ice water and a Jack and Coke in front of him.

He kept going over in his head how not to act too desperate. If he looked desperate, and talked desperate, he'd look weak and Arkady would pass. He'd seen such rookie mistakes a hundred times. He'd even done it himself, in his salad days. The Russians didn't need to know how badly he needed the business.

When the man in black with the pronounced nose approached the table, Trent, all smiles, rose with an extended hand.

"Hello, Alexander, it's great to finally see you."

"Mr. Trent, good evening."

Trent didn't break stride. He waved over the passing waiter and Arkady ordered coffee. They sat down.

"You want to spice that joe with something stronger?" Trent asked.

"I don't drink alcohol."

"I started sneaking Dad's whiskey when I was ten and we were fishing on weekends." Trent let out a low laugh and hoped it didn't sound forced. It sure felt forced. But he was glad he had the story to tell. He'd needed to think back on fishing stories because his research showed Arkady liked to fish, too. "I hear you're an excellent fisherman yourself," Trent added, seeding the conversation.

Arkady's coffee arrived. The Hawk finally cracked a smile. "My grandfather taught me to fish. My mother and I lived with him."

"What about your father?"

Arkady shrugged. "He was killed overseas."

"I'm sorry."

"He was a patriot and we buried him with honors," Arkady said, "and his legacy put me where I am today. I had a fine upbringing. My best catch, *ever*, was a seven-pound bass my president and I caught while on a US visit. He didn't catch anything near that size, so he 'borrowed' it for a photo op."

Trent suppressed a laugh when he realized Arkady was no longer smiling. He didn't think he'd be doing a great deal of smiling around the Hawk.

"Bet it tasted great," Trent said.

"There is no better seafood than fresh-caught bass."

"I hear the salmon at this place is good," Trent said, consulting the menu. "The sky is the limit, anything you want."

Arkady examined the menu, flipping pages. "You fish when not working?"

"Oh, when my father passed, I pretty much gave up fishing. I got into model railroading after that."

Arkady lowered the menu, eyebrows raised. "Really? I have a railroad set at my home. Wonderful pastime."

"When you visit my place in Texas, I'll show you mine. I have a room with three train layouts. I get lost in there for days."

Arkady smiled and his eyes genuinely lit up. Trent felt a calm fall over him. Finally breaking the ice, and the Russian seemed to be made of ice, inside and out, meant they would have a good conversation. They'd found common ground not once, but twice. Trent had learned early on that if you can make a potential customer a friend instead of somebody you're selling to, they'll buy whatever you have to offer, even if they want to do a little horse-trading before deciding on the final number.

Trent returned his attention to the menu. "The sirloin sure sounds nice."

"I may just try the salmon you speak so highly of, Mr. Trent."

"Please, call me Theo."

Arkady lowered the menu to lean forward a little. "I think we'll get along just fine, Theo."

Trent nodded. There was still no guarantee that the Russian would buy his weapon, but he was closer to a deal now more than ever. He'd save his company, his legacy, and not feel like a failure.

And he'd already decided that, once the company was flush and on track, he'd tell Colleen to forge her own path. She'd attached herself to him long enough. She deserved a life of her own.

"Well he sure cracked that Russian iceberg fast," Dane said.

He and Nina sat in a corner booth of the steakhouse with a view of Trent's table. The booth had the advantage of being out of range of the general lighting in the dining area. A flickering candle provided the light they had, which meant Trent and his guest couldn't see them.

"I'm stunned," Nina said. "That's the Hawk."

"Who?"

"Alexander Arkady, Putin's 'fixer'. All the dirty jobs go to him. Colder than Butte, Montana, in the dead of winter."

"Did you work with him?"

"Yup."

"Better put a bag over your head."

"It's been long enough that he won't recognize me."

"Wanna bet?"

"You might be right. His crew had a nickname for me."

"Dare I ask?"

"Let's save that for the exciting climax," Nina said.

"What are they talking about?"

"Whatever it is, you can bet Arkady's on a mission. And that means he doesn't have anybody's interest in mind but Russia's."

"Which means Putin."

"Russia is Putin. Yup. Pooty-Poot is up to no good, as usual, and your country is dumb enough to let him get away with it."

Dane said, "I'm not."

"Sure you aren't."

"Is Trent in danger?"

"Not now. They need him. Later, perhaps, when they no longer do. But that could be weeks, months, years from now. He's safe in the meantime."

"Nothing ever changes in Russia," Dane said.

"Just the names, dear," she said.

The food arrived and the strong aromas awoke an appetite Trent didn't realize he had. He cut into the fillet with gusto as the waiter refilled Arkady's coffee and brought Trent another Jack and Coke. "Tell me more about your device," the Hawk said.

He's on the hook. Don't confuse him with too much jargon. "Basically," Trent said, "my weapon sends a concentration of focused energy at a target. Your people worked on particle-beam technology in the '70s and '80s, right?"

"It was unstable and too expensive."

"But you're familiar with the concept."

"We are. How is direct energy different?"

"We're not using electromagnetic fields to produce the energy burst," Trent said. "That's where your instability came from. Too much juice and not enough control. Particle beams are like trying to pour a glass of water into an empty milk jug. Not all of it gets in the opening, the water spills all over, and you end up with a mess. Direct energy is using a glass of water to fill that milk jug, but you have a funnel to guide the water in. No mess. The downside is a delay in the actual discharge. Direct energy needs to build up pressure, so to speak, which is then released in a concentrated form that blows up the target."

"I don't understand," the Russian said, and chewed a small piece of salmon. His eyes stayed focused on Trent.

"Say you have a pipe controlling the flow of water or steam. Steam might be a better example. The steam needs to vent. If something blocks that ventilation, pressure builds. Eventually the pipe or a blow-off valve lets go and you have to plug the rupture.

"My DEW works the same way. The exact system is classified, but when the weapon is activated, the stored energy builds to a level where it finally shoots out at a target. Inside the machine we have six lasers that concentrate into one beam, like the Death Star in *Star Wars*."

"I don't watch movies."

Trent laughed. "I'll show you how it works in a video. You can't see the beams, but I can describe it. Now, this weapon will give you an incredible advantage on the battlefield. You already know, I'm sure, that the US Navy has a similar weapon on some ships, but this will be one you can deploy on the ground.

"We're talking speed-of-light engagement," Trent continued. "For the first shot, the energy needs to build up, takes a few seconds. Follow-up shots are faster. You can operate with two guys in a truck, but we're working on a movable platform and, of course, making the components smaller."

"What about collateral damage?"

"Almost none. When you have a pinpoint beam, there's no missile or shell to go astray. Cheap, too. About a dollar a shot. Have you seen the cost of a missile lately?"

The Hawk shrugged.

"The beam, by the way, is really slick. Three nanometers in diameter."

"I have no idea what a nanometer is."

"It's one billionth of a meter. Let's just say it's very thin. Take the thinnest piece of thread you can find, and it's thinner than that. Like I said, aim at the target, hit only the target."

"What range?"

"About a mile."

"That's not terrible."

"Not as good as we'd like, but the science, right now, says we can't go any further without creating the instability of the old particle beams."

Arkady nodded. Trent chewed his steak and looked over the Hawk's shoulder at a tall man coming quickly to their table. The man did not look happy, his face a tough mask, and Trent recognized the laptop bag he carried. *His own!*

"Who is this?"

Arkady turned to look. "Marco?"

Cavallos, carrying the laptop case, pulled over an empty neighboring over and sat down. He placed the bag on the table and turned to Trent.

"Be more careful," Cavallos said. Then to Arkady, "Somebody broke into the room and started cracking the safe."

"And?"

"The thief is quite dead."

Cavallos glared at Trent once again before leaving. The fire in the man's dark eyes chilled Trent head to toe. That man was a killer. He'd probably killed the thief, which meant there was a dead body up in his room, and he'd have to report what happened. He'd have to find a way to explain why the man had been shot. Trent had no weapons with which to shoot anybody, that was the only thing that would clear him of suspicion, but the situation all around would tie him up for days. And ruin the deal with the Russian.

The laptop case remained on the table.

Trent's appetite vanished. He put down his fork. It made a loud clang against the plate. "What does—"

Arkady waved off the comment and ate some more. Trent stared at the man. He didn't seem bothered in the least. He was Ice Man again.

"This is what happens when you anger your country, Theo."

Trent tried to reply, but the words stuck in his mouth.

Chapter Twenty-One

"That was interesting," Nina said.

"Marco Cavallos," Dane said. "Reporting to your Russian friend, how nice."

"Never heard of him."

"He and his wife are freelance do-anything mercenaries who ran with Spanish anarchists way back when. Sort of the bad-guy version of you and me, except the woman doesn't talk as much."

She kicked him under the table. Dane stifled a groan and ate a piece of steak and tried not to laugh.

"I think something awful has happened to our friend Blaze," Dane said.

Nina sipped her wine. "Uh-huh."

"Shame. Two mil would have been nice."

"Should we find out what makes his murder worthwhile? Maybe blow up some laser guns? Stop the Russian from acquiring the technology?"

"Sure," Dane said. "It'll be like the Cold War never ended."

"It didn't," Nina said.

Dane raised an eyebrow.

"For *us*," she added.

Dane didn't reply.

Trent, shaken by the news, was in no shape to finish the dinner
meeting.

Of all the complications he could plan for, murder
certainly wasn't one of them.

Angered his country? He wasn't doing anything illegal! The US government may not approve, but they had
no authority over who he did business with as long as he
wasn't violating the law.

Arkady paid the check and, holding on to the laptop
case, led Trent back to his room. The Texan stood frozen
in the hall. Despite selling weapons to the government,
he'd never been in war. Never fired a gun in anger. The
only dead things he'd seen were deer he shot or spiders he
smashed. A dead body was totally new, and he figured it
would look nothing like what he saw in the movies and on
television. Arkady took Trent's key card and opened the
door. The smell hit them first. Arkady grabbed Trent's right
elbow and pushed him into the room. Trent leaned against
the bathroom doorway. His knees felt weak.

"Here's what happened," Arkady said. The Hawk
moved around the room with ease, almost ignoring the
dead man on the floor and the blood soaking into the carpet. "Our friend had a partner. They cracked the safe and
one shot the other, escaping with your documents."

The blood drained from Trent's face. "But—"

"It has to be reported that the documents were stolen.
Your government has to believe it was a successful robbery. Then they will hunt for the other thief."

"But—"

"Trust me, Theo. This sort of thing is my job. Now, pick up the phone and report this. Don't be afraid of the police. I'll come see you in a few hours."

Trent moved on weak knees to the bed. He had to tip-toe around the body to keep from stepping in blood. Not much of the carpet remained untouched by the growing pool. He kept his eyes purposefully away from the dead man too. Sitting on the bed, he was at least facing away from the body.

"Don't take too long, Theo," Arkady said as he slipped out.

The door shut. The silence in the room quickly became unbearable. Trent was all alone.

Maybe Colleen was right. I should have listened.

He picked up the phone.

Within minutes of his call to the desk, security flooded Trent's room, everybody excited and speaking hurriedly in French, with Trent in a corner giving a statement to the only member of the security staff who spoke English. When the police finally arrived, he gave his statement again, seeing Arkady in his mind's eye as he spoke, following the Russian's coaching to the last word. He even started to believe it himself.

Hotel security hustled Trent to another room and left him there. He was not allowed to collect personal belongings until the police finished. It appeared quite open and shut, so sorry for the trouble, they said.

Trouble indeed.

But at least he still had his laptop and documents. He'd held onto the case the whole time in his room.

He grabbed a small bottle of Jim Beam from the room's mini-fridge and drank down the bourbon in two throws. Gasping, he sat on the bed and stared at the carpet. There was no blood on the carpet and somehow that surprised him.

All he'd wanted to do was make a sale, and now a man was dead. Had his own government really sent the thief? The State Department had indeed paid a visit prior to his trip, and they had seemed upset when he told them he wouldn't cancel the meeting.

If the US government were trying to sabotage him, it only strengthened his resolve. Who were they to say with whom he could do business? And if the Pentagon had made a deal, all this could have been avoided.

The thief's death was on them.

But the incident showed that the Russians were quite unorthodox. The man who had visited the table had not been Russian. A contractor? Whoever he was, Arkady's order had been "shoot first."

Which meant they wanted to buy. Nobody brought in that kind of muscle simply to kick tires.

Trent let out a breath and kicked off his shoes.

Cavallos opened the door for Arkady. The Hawk entered.

Roxana lay on the bed, in her bathrobe, reading a magazine. Her hair was still wet.

"Enjoying your evening?" Arkady said.

"What do you need?" Cavallos said.

The Hawk snapped his attention to the male part of the team. "Excellent work tonight. I have suggested to Trent that his own government was responsible, that the intruder had a partner that shot him, and he will rely on me to smooth his way forward."

"What's next?"

"That's what I am here to talk about. You're going to

Texas, like I said earlier."

Roxana put down her magazine as she listened to the Hawk's update.

The next day Dane and Nina rose early and opened the window to let in the morning air. The sun burned high and highlighted the blue ocean and cloudless sky. The pool was full of kids, sunbathers on either side.

Dane ordered bacon and eggs for breakfast while Nina showered.

He sat at the table looking out at the water. The distance concealed the chaos of the crashing waves. They had stumbled onto something big, and no mistake. Whatever had happened in Trent's room, the hotel had kept it quiet, and he wasn't sure it was all over. Dane looked forward to seeing if Arkady and Trent were still at the hotel. If each party left quickly, he and Nina had to start figuring where they'd go. Dane had an idea, and research on his phone pinned his thoughts to the bull's eye. If the Russians were going to buy Trent's weapon, they'd have to travel to his headquarters in Corpus Christi, Texas.

Breakfast arrived. The blonde woman pushed a cart with dishes atop into the room. She helped Dane set the table. When they finished, he asked if she spoke English. Yes, she did. Dane handed her a significant tip and asked why hotel security had been in such a big powwow with the local cops last night.

The woman hesitated.

"Is that not enough?" Dane said.

She looked at the bill and then back at Dane.

He was, of course, taking a shot in the dark. She might not know anything. But hotel staff all over the world gossiped like mad. She *had* to know something.

"An incident, *monsieur*. A man was shot in a room. They say he was stealing something."

Dane thanked her with a bonus and shut the door behind her. He knocked on the bathroom door, shouted, "Breakfast!" and went to the table to dig into the bacon and eggs. Nina came out in her bathrobe with a towel wrapped around her head. She sat and started eating.

"Blaze has left this world to sit with his fathers," Dane said.

"I figured." She swallowed some food. "What are you thinking?"

"Trent and Arkady might leave right away."

"I certainly would." Her fork scraped against the plate as she scooped up more eggs. She ate hunched over, in a hurry, as if somebody was going to steal her food.

"You okay?" Dane said.

"Sure."

"You wandered out of bed last night."

"I needed a walk."

"Another nightmare?"

She remained over her plate but raised her eyes. "What about it?"

"I'm concerned, that's all."

She put her fork down and sat back. She folded her arms. "Yes, another nightmare. I couldn't get back to sleep and didn't want to wake you up so I took a walk."

Dane nodded. Her movement had woken him up. He figured another dream had disturbed her and didn't stop her from leaving because everybody needs their own space from time to time.

"Did seeing Arkady trigger something?"

"Maybe."

"Dammit, Nina."

"It's private, okay? I don't want to talk about it. Can I finish my breakfast now?"

"*May* I finish my breakfast now."

"You ass." She dug back into her food.

Dane let the silence between them grow a bit, and then she said, "So what's the plan, Mr. Know-It-All?"

"If Trent and the Russian leave now, which I suspect they will, I think they'll go straight to Corpus Cristi."

"Where's that?"

"Texas," he said. "Trent's headquarters is there. Presumably, so is his laser gun."

"Let's go to Texas." *Scrape, swallow.* "See what they do next." She grabbed a piece of toast to pick up the stray pieces of egg on her plate.

"Yup."

"Now something's bothering *you*," she said, biting off a large piece of toast. She wiped her mouth with the back of her hand.

"This one isn't right," Dane said. "They brought in assassins to help with a business deal. And now everybody's going to Texas."

"Who was Trent's competition? The one he lost the contract to."

"We'll find out. I'll get on the computer when we finish."

"You mean I'll help you on the computer when we finish."

"I can do *some* things," Dane said.

"Solitaire hardly counts as a computer skill."

They ate quietly for a while, the amount of food shrinking by the minute. Nina said, "Arkady was very good at sabotage and propaganda. He may have designs on the competition, too. And if he's just going to write

Trent a check and call it a day, I'm selling a condo on the moon."

"I have a feeling you're right, but what exactly do they have in mind? That's what we need to learn and stop."

"Think there's any money in it?"

"Oh, probably not." Dane chewed some toast. "We'll have to finance it on our own, if you haven't gambled away all our money."

"Usually you say *my* money."

"I'm working on my sharing skills."

She laughed. He smiled.

"When we get to the US," Nina said, "why don't you look up the competition and I'll find a way to get chummy with Trent. Pose as a reporter or something."

"You aren't going to try and seduce him, are you?"

"Of course not. I don't like old guys."

Chapter Twenty-Two

Arkady contacted Trent around 10:00 a.m. and told him to get to Texas ASAP. The Hawk added that he'd be taking his private jet and his flight was leaving at noon.

Trent talked with hotel security, only to be told that his belongings were still off-limits, as they were part of the crime scene. When he told them he had to leave, they made arrangements to ship his clothes and other items to his home.

At least he had his laptop, blueprints and pictures.

Trent booked a late-afternoon flight, which cost almost double since it was last minute. He didn't care. He wanted to finish the deal with the Russians and get on with his life, if that was indeed possible. If his own government was working against him, he might lose his company despite selling to the Russians. After all these years, when he thought he was at the top of his game, he now faced an abyss from which he feared he wouldn't return.

Alexander Arkady unbuckled his seat belt as the private jet reached cruising altitude. He was happy to leave Monaco and very excited for the next phase. The plane's hostess brought him a mug of coffee, and he asked her to step into the flight cabin while he made a phone call.

President Putin's assistant answered on the third ring.

"I need him," Arkady said.

A moment later Putin came on the line.

"Am I disturbing you, sir?"

"Perfect timing. I've been wondering about your progress."

"We have a reason to be pleased but also cautious," Arkady said. He explained his dinner with Trent and the attempted robbery, and how Cavallos and his wife had foiled the attempt, leaving the suspect dead in Trent's hotel room.

"You seriously think it was the Americans?" Putin said.

"The police identified the thief as John Blaze, remember him?"

"I do."

"He may have been working on his own, but I think the coincidence is too much."

"Our people in Washington haven't mentioned any covert moves against Trent."

"Unless he learned about the meeting through some loose-lip gossiper on Trent's side of the deal, I think we can bet surely on the US government hiring a stringer."

Putin didn't respond to the advisory. Arkady hadn't expected him to. But he knew the words had settled into his boss's mind. "How is Trent?" the Russian premier said.

"Shaken enough that he can be manipulated properly, if I don't push too hard."

"Make sure you apply only *necessary* pressure, Alexander."

"When we reach Texas and his home soil, I think he will calm down, but he trusts me. You should have seen him hanging on my every word in the hotel, sir."

Putin let out a soft chuckle. "Do you need anything else?"

"I'd like another assistant for when I send Cavallos to Hess Laboratories. Can you send Ivanov?"

"I will order him personally."

"Please tell him to bring his knives."

"I will. Good work so far; may your good fortune continue, comrade."

"Thank you, comrade."

It felt good to say the word again.

Dane and Nina's plane touched down in Texas a little over fourteen hours later. She'd slept most of the way across the ocean, while Dane remained awake. He watched her, noting how peaceful she looked, and hoped there weren't any demons screaming in her head.

Customs took almost an hour, with their passports and luggage selected for thorough review, sleepy-eyed Nina more quiet than usual.

Unlike his previous two visits to the United States, this time Dane was traveling under an alias. He would not trip alarms in Washington, DC or at the FBI or CIA. The last thing he needed was official government agents inquiring about his visit. They'd all know that if he was there, he was chasing trouble, the kind of trouble that more often than not involved high stakes. Dane needed a free hand this time. He'd call the cavalry when the time was right. The government did not approve of his activities in general and didn't like it when he worked in the US in particular. He'd meddled in CIA business enough to earn the extra attention, but he also had a few allies who understood he looked out for the underdog no matter how many toes he stepped on.

There were more who disliked him for other reasons, because of his father's alleged betrayal of the country. Why they blamed him, Dane had no idea. It was best to stay off the radar in the meantime.

The customs officer found his passport in complete order and allowed him through.

Nina was traveling under a cover identity as well, since her name would sound the same alarms as Dane's. They were known to be joined at the hip.

Dane rented a car, a hot Jaguar F-Type for which he paid a high premium. It was his current favorite vehicle, but he never drove enough to justify owning one. He certainly wasn't going to drive about in a standard automobile. In case the action turned heavy, they'd need a fast machine that could take a corner like a train on rails. The standard rental couldn't handle that duty. Dane only wished the Jag had a standard-shift transmission instead of the electronic paddle-shift mechanism on the back of the steering wheel. The one consolation to that was at least new computer-controlled transmissions shifted faster than even a professional race driver could shift a standard.

The busy city was a shock after the luxurious tranquility of Monaco. They sat in traffic for thirty minutes trying to get to their hotel. When they finally checked in, Nina dropped her bags on the bed and flopped onto the mattress.

"It's hot in here," she said.

Dane went to the wall and turned on the air conditioner. It blew loudly but filled the room with cold air very quickly.

"Now it's blowing right on me," Nina said.

"Are you going to complain all day?"

"I haven't even started, sweetie."

Chapter Twenty-Three

Dane unpacked and hung up his clothes, but everything needed dry cleaning and pressing. He made a mental note to take care of that in the morning and told Nina to set out whatever she wanted cleaned, too. The hotel had a guest laundry room for their other clothes.

No balcony but the window looked out on the city. No smoking, either. Welcome to the US. Dane selected a can of Coors from the mini-fridge and slouched in a chair.

"We need to recon Trent's place," he said.

Nina remained flat on her back, eyes on the ceiling. "Uh-huh."

Dane took a drink. Coors wasn't his preferred beer. He hardly drank beer at all. But it sure tasted good.

"We can do that tomorrow," he said. "Tonight, I want to go over your idea for getting in touch with Trent."

"Sure."

"You realize that Hess Laboratories is in Florida, right?"

More research via the airline's not-for-free WiFi revealed Hess Laboratories as Trent's competitor.

"Yes," she said.

"I'll have to fly out there for that part of the job." He drank some more Coors.

"You have to call me every day," she said.

"Uh-huh."

"I'm serious."

"I will."

"Promise?"

"Yes, darling."

"Good." She rolled off the bed, stretched her arms to the ceiling, arching her back as she did so. She began taking off her clothes. "I need a shower," she said, as her last undergarment hit the floor. She headed for the bathroom. Her dimpled rear end jiggled as she walked. Dane followed the view subtly.

"Come help me wash my hair," she said.

Dane left the beer on the table.

Following the Jag's GPS, the top down and the brilliant Texas sun burning down on them, Dane steered along the curving mountain road. Considering the smoothness of the asphalt, it wasn't heavily traveled. The lack of bumps didn't matter. The Jag's taut suspension created a rough ride. Dane did have to slow for a crossing squirrel now and then.

The hills were alive with green grass and trees, and as they climbed higher, the sprawling valley below grew. Dane finally pulled over when the Trent Defense complex appeared. The back acreage of the campus, its dusty brown contrasting with the green, seemed out of place.

"Nice place to work," Nina said. "I bet they have a wonderful cafeteria."

"I'm sure Trent provides his employees with nothing."

"Nothing?"

"But the best, of course. Doesn't every corporation?"

"Sometimes I can't tell if you're a communist or a fascist."

Dane laughed. "I'm just a cynic."

He had a right to be, he thought, especially about his homeland. He'd left the CIA and ultimately the US under a cloud of suspicion because of the allegations of betrayal that landed on his father, and the man's resulting suicide. But he remained loyal to allies still loyal to him. Not everybody had the president on speed dial. Dane did. President Peter Cross was one such ally with whom Dane remained close and was one of the few who knew for certain that the cloud under which he had left was not his fault.

Dane opened a pouch containing binoculars and lifted them to his eyes. To access the main building of Trent Defense meant first stopping at a guard post at the front gate. Dane saw that the guard was not armed.

He scanned the length of the main building and then the perimeter fence. Security implements were not obvious, but since Trent did defense work for the government, Dane imagined there was an armed force ready to pounce if needed, and that pressure sensors in the ground would announce unauthorized intruders.

Which made it all the more chilling that Trent was going to escort Arkady onto the property.

"Let me see," Nina said.

Dane passed her the binoculars and gave his impression as she looked.

"No testing going on today."

A welcome breeze rustled the surrounding grass.

"They're gonna save that for when the Russians get here."

"Uh-huh."

Dane started the car and executed a slow U-turn and

followed the mountain road to where it intersected with the road leading to the campus. He turned right. The straight two-lane blacktop led to the outer edge of the city, a busy couple of blocks with shops, restaurants and office buildings.

Dane parked the Jag on the street, and he and Nina walked hand in hand along the sidewalk, passing shop fronts and pedestrians going about their day. They stopped at an outdoor café and ordered lunch. Nina took out her phone and cycled through some photographs, stopping when she came to a picture of Trent's daughter, Colleen. The image was from a profile article in the city newspaper highlighting the assumed heir to Trent's empire.

"Think she'll be around?" Nina said.

Dane took the phone and looked at the photo.

"I figure any employee not eating at Trent's wonderful cafeteria will come down here for lunch."

"You're mocking me."

Dane grinned. "Just a little."

The waiter brought their sandwiches and two bottles of cold sparkling water. Dane ordered hot roast beef while Nina selected the house special, a turkey breast with cran-berry spread, house mustard and veggies.

"Maybe you should go to Florida," he said. "I'll stay here and seduce the daughter for information."

Nina snatched back the phone.

"Do that and I'll turn you into a eunuch."

Dane ignored Nina's glare and bit into his sandwich.

They finished thirty minutes later but remained to watch the street. The lunch rush filled the café and faded an hour later, but they saw no sign of Colleen Trent at the café or any of the surrounding restaurants.

When they returned to the Jag, Dane said, "Do you

think the daughter could help?"

"I read the profile a few times. She's entrenched in her father's work but said she'd like to see them expand into areas other than defense. She's young enough to be an idealist but still knows where her bread is buttered."

"So that's a yes?"

"Yes. If we can convince her that Arkady means to do her father harm, which I'm sure of, she'll help."

"How are you sure?"

"Arkady is a hardline communist. The dirty-tricks expert. Every dirty job, remember? He has something in mind. We just have to find out what."

Dane started the car and drove back to the hotel.

Chapter Twenty-Four

Nina sat on the bed clicking through TV channels while Dane sat on the edge and dialed Todd McConn.

"Can you come out and play?" he said.

"Sure."

"Fly down to Florida and start prelim work on Hess Laboratories. I'll join you tomorrow."

"Where are you now?"

"Corpus Christi. We just looked at Trent's property." He explained their activities so far.

"This sounds like a fun one," McConn said. "I think I'll pack an extra bag of tricks."

"I trust you to handle that."

"See you soon, Steve."

Dane ended the call.

"This is ridiculous," Nina said.

"What?"

"There's nothing to watch and there are only fifteen channels. I keep hearing Americans enjoy seven hundred channels. Is that a lie?"

"It's not a lie, and even if we did have seven hundred

channels, there'd still be nothing to watch."

She scooted over to make room for Dane, and he stretched out next to her. He felt the warmth of her body through her clothes.

They settled on a reality show about a group of people who argued over storage shed auctions. The men were overweight and the women subservient. All acted about as smart as a box of rocks. Dane could only shake his head at a country that turned such walking disasters into entertainment. His sanity was well preserved by not participating in such useless shenanigans.

Later they had dinner sent up and turned off the TV.

Dane went out before room service arrived and purchased two candles. They ate by candlelight and turned in early. Dane planned to pick up the dry cleaning in the morning before leaving for Florida.

Nine drove him to the airport the next morning and kissed him good-bye. He told her to be careful.

On the flight, a sudden restlessness overtook him and he had a hard time sitting still. He hated to leave her alone, with her nightmares, because that's why she became anxious and drank. She'd drink anyway, but without him, more than usual. But he also plain hated being away from her.

Worse, he had no idea how to make the nightmares stop.

The three elderly men in charge of The Trust met in a park in down-town Zurich, Switzerland, where one of the operations hubs of their organization was located.

Number One fed breadcrumbs to pigeons while seated on a bench. Number Two showed up with a poodle on a leash. Number Three arrived carrying only a shopping bag.

"Isn't this cute," Number One said. "Three old-timers in

a park." A handful of breadcrumbs was quickly consumed by the cooing pigeons.

Number Two picked up his poodle, who wanted some of the crumbs for himself, and growled when the opportunity was taken from him.

"Bad news about Monaco," Two said.

"Yes. Blaze was a good man. He will be impossible to replace even if we recruit ten more people."

"Arkady is with Trent in Texas now," Two said. "If we do not carefully plan our next steps, the Russians will buy his weapon system. What are we going to do to stop them?"

"I was hoping one of you," Number One said, "might have a suggestion."

Three spoke up. "We checked the registered guests at the hotel. Two names jumped out."

"Who?"

"Steve Dane and Nina Talikova."

"Really?" Number One raised an eyebrow. He tossed more breadcrumbs. "Do we know where they are now?"

"They are no longer in Monaco," Three said. "There is also no sign of them in Texas, but that doesn't mean they aren't there."

"If Dane and Talikova witnessed anything that happened in Monaco," Number One said, "you know they will be interested in following up."

Two said, "They may solve our Blaze problem."

"Indeed," Number One said. "And perhaps we can entice them into the organization."

"They won't join," Three said.

"Don't be so sure," One said.

"What carrot will you dangle?" Three said.

"We can always tell Dane the truth about his father. That would certainly motivate him to cooperate."

The pigeons cooed as they waited at the feet of Number One for more breadcrumbs.

Colleen Trent parked her car in the company lot and shut off the engine. She took a deep breath as she gathered her purse and briefcase from the passenger seat.

Exiting the car, she started toward the building.

Her father was home. That pleased her. She had not spoken with him since his return, so she expected a full update when they saw each other.

Had he even watched her medical presentation?

He wasn't one to lie to her so perhaps he had. Since they hadn't talked, there was no way to know for sure. She'd have to ask him. And if he hadn't watched, she'd ask him why.

There was no way she was going to let the topic go without an argument.

There had to be a better way to make a living than selling death.

She'd had no qualms about making weapons for the defense of her country. She trusted the government and military to only use those weapons when a pressing need required their use. But another country? One that had shown aggression to other parts of the world, such as Russia, in recent months? No. She had to fight this one.

She entered the building and found her office as quiet as she'd left it the night before. There were no decorations or other items to make it more like home. She hadn't joined her father to stay long, so she hadn't bothered. But she had stayed long, much longer than anticipated, and she wondered if she'd ever break away. They needed each other. More truthfully, she needed him. The death of her mother still weighed on her a great deal.

As soon as she stepped into her office, colleagues began asking about her father. He wasn't answering his phone at home and hadn't shown up.

Colleen Trent did not take the news well. She went from zero to panic very quickly. This wasn't like him at all. She'd only received a text message from him saying that he was home, but they hadn't talked the night before.

She tried the home line. Nothing. Hanging up, she grabbed her purse and said she'd go to the house and personally check on him.

Nobody stopped her.

Chapter Twenty-Five

Theodore Trent's home office occupied a room on the second floor, down the hall from the master bedroom with a smaller bedroom and bath in between.

The window behind his desk looked out on the large backyard and pool he never used but on which he spent a lot of money on upkeep. Colleen used it maybe three or four times a month for exercise, but he'd yet to so much as dip a toe into the water. He considered the pool a decoration.

His home office retained the bare essentials same as Trent Defense HQ. The empty fish tank against one wall was a memorial to a time when he'd tried to dress the place up a little. Instead, he'd killed the fish.

Colleen knocked on the door.

The knock snapped him out of a daze. He'd been staring at nothing for a long time as his mind continued to process what had happened in Monaco.

He gave the notes and papers on his desk an absent-minded glance as he told his daughter to enter. He needed to keep what happened from her; he needed to pretend he was his normal self. Colleen approached the desk, and concern flashed across her face.

"What's wrong?" she said.

"I'm still a little jet-lagged. Hard to concentrate. Why aren't you at the office?"

"You haven't shown up and you won't answer your phone. Everybody's asking about you. So here I am."

"I don't need any distractions today, Colleen." Trent sat down.

"Did something go wrong with your meeting?"

Oh, yes, he thought.

"No," he said. "In fact, I think we have a deal."

"I thought that's what you wanted. You don't seem very excited."

"Jet lag."

She finally sat down on the chair in front of his desk and leaned forward a little. "What's next?"

"Our Russian friend is coming here. I want to do a big dinner. You, me, some top-level people from the project." He handed her a page of notes. "You're in charge. See if you can get the same chef we had the last time, um…"

"Higgins."

"Right, that guy."

"Anything else?"

"No, that's all. Tell everybody."

"Dad, my presentation?"

He let out a breath. "Of course, honey, I forgot."

"You didn't see it?"

"I watched it on the flight, as I promised. I watched every second of it."

"But you think it's stupid."

"Not at all. I honestly don't know the first thing about how to do it."

"You think it will work?"

"All I've ever done is military stuff, honey. I'm an old dog and you're trying to teach me a new trick."

"There's nothing to be afraid of," she said. "There are consultants and all kinds of people—"

He leaned forward so fast she pulled back. "Colleen, there's no investment money. No money for retooling or new hires. My usual funding sources are the same as me. We know one thing. I would need to find investors with your level of understanding. We simply cannot afford that right now."

"But, Dad—"

"If I don't close this deal, we're finished. I haven't wanted to tell you this, but I must. If we fail to sell the weapon, there is no more Trent Defense. I retire and the building closes and you and everybody else—"

"Any other corporation wouldn't bother if it was this bad. They'd close the doors and the hell with everybody."

"And that's a sad commentary on our culture, isn't it? I'm trying to do the right thing. For all of us."

Colleen stared at her father. Finally, she said, "I'll get started on the dinner prep." She rose from the chair.

"Colleen."

But he was talking to her back. Then she was out the door and gone.

Trent put his head in his hands. The right thing? For everybody? One man dead already and who knew what was coming next. Arkady blamed the Feds. Was he right, or was this some kind of old-style Soviet trickery? Plenty of Russians, ones like Arkady, were old dogs, too.

What have I done?

If things went south, if another attempt at theft or sabotage occurred, there was only one thing to do. Stop the deal and take his chances. Be like every other corporation. Walk away with his golden parachute.

He had never envisioned his career ending that way. Trent sat up, a sense of resolve coming over him. He'd never caved before and he wasn't going to now. Let them come. Whoever they were. He'd finish this deal and throw it right back in their faces, and if the Feds cut him off, well…Colleen had some great ideas. The future of the company was in good hands.

Colleen returned to her office in a huff. She assured the executives and her colleagues that her father was at home and taking care of business after a good meeting overseas, finished most of her work, and left before five. The notes about the dinner remained on her desk.

She collected her mail and slammed the apartment door a little harder than intended, the impact knocking a framed photo off a nearby shelf. She picked up the frame. The photo showed her and her father, when she was ten, fishing from his old boat. She was holding up a fish for the camera with a gap-toothed smile, wearing a hat too big for her head that almost covered her eyes. Dad was beaming behind her, hatless. He'd given her his hat so she didn't get a sunburn. She'd forgotten her own at home.

They'd stopped fishing after grandpa had died. Colleen would have liked to keep the tradition going, but her father said he wasn't able to, at least "not right now, maybe someday" but "not right now, maybe someday" had turned into "never again" and she missed the good times they'd shared.

Colleen replaced the picture and changed into jeans and a sweater. Sitting at the computer nook in one corner of the living room, she ignored the growling in her stomach and logged on to the company network. Using her father's password, she opened the directory containing the company's financial information.

She sorted through the files, making notes and jotting numbers, and when she logged off, she looked at her notes and numbers and then stared at the wall with folded arms, lips pressed tightly together.

Dad wasn't making it up, and the math didn't lie. Trent Defense had enough cash to cover overhead for two more months. That was all that was all that was left. Her father's personal account was okay. He could retire, no problem. His employees would move on if the company closed. That's life and sometimes you get a bad hand.

But her father saw retirement as the first stage of death. It wasn't just the employees he was thinking of, despite his rhetoric.

Failure would destroy him.

Okay, then. Close the deal with the Russians. Bring up retooling again once the dust settled and the accounts were flush.

Her stomach growled again. Colleen left the computer and went to the kitchen.

While she prepared dinner, she wondered if a closing wasn't all that bad after all. Dad had his trains to occupy his attention, as well as fishing. He wouldn't sit around and waste away to nothing.

And maybe if the company closed, she might find a new direction in her own life. Colleen hadn't intended on staying so close to her father. She'd studied the math and science necessary to land a solid engineering job because his passion became her passion, the apple didn't far fall from the tree, all that, but after her mother died, her father seemed so alone in the world that she couldn't stand the thought of leaving Texas.

Maybe now her time to leave the nest had finally arrived. She wasn't getting any younger, and it might be nice to settle down and find a husband. The quiet apartment sometimes suffocated her, a reminder of her lack of a love life, her barely-there social life, and all the wants and needs she had set aside to take care of Dad. She hadn't bothered to buy a pet. Maybe a cat would be nice to have.

She seasoned a piece of steak as a pan warmed. She decided, yeah, a closing might give everybody a fresh start. Her father would not accept such counsel. The Russian deal was going to go through, like it or not, and they'd take their chances. Maybe when it was all done, she'd pack up and leave anyway.

It was time.

Chapter Twenty-Six

Halfway around the world, The Trust met in a secured video conference on the dark web. From his office in Zurich, Number One faced his two colleagues on the desktop computer screen. The large desk was empty of clutter except for decorations around the edge, including a cigar humidor he did not open. Dark carpeting matched the color of the walls, curtains over the window danced inward with each gust of wind.

"It's confirmed," he told the other two. "Monaco police have Blaze's body in the morgue."

"We've failed on that phase," said Number Three. "What about our other people?"

"I say we pull them out, because Blaze's death revealed another element that could work to our advantage. There were two people at the casino that we've had our eyes on for some time. Stephen Dane and Nina Talikova."

"Really?" Number Two said. "We might still have a chance if we can recruit those two."

"We know that Trent and Arkady are now in Texas," said Number One. "Dane and Talikova are no longer in

Monaco, but we have no record of their entry into the US. That doesn't mean they aren't there."

"You're suggesting Dane's dealt himself in," Number Three said. "We can't assume—"

"We know enough about Dane to know he'd get involved if he was able to sniff out a problem. The Russian woman would certainly recognize Arkady. We can have our people looking for them. But they may already be in Texas. If so, it's only a matter of time before they turn up, and I suggest we finally make an approach."

"I'll alert our people in Texas," Number Two said. "But will we have enough to entice Dane to join us?"

"We do," said Number One. "We have the answers to questions he's been asking for a long time. Answers to questions about what happened to his father."

The knives gleamed in the afternoon sun, their stainless-steel blades razor-sharp. Yuri Gregorovitch Ivanov addressed the knives mentally while on his knees before them. They were his friends, his tools. He did not like guns. He'd learned to use knives and make them as deadly as a gun. The knives were Ivanov's trademark.

Birds chirped in the quiet forest Ivanov occupied. His paper target, posted on a tree stump, waited twenty yards ahead. Ivanov, a bulky Cossack with a thick chest and wide shoulders, lifted his head to the target. He tuned out the birds and the rustle of the trees. He was one with his knives.

He collected all six blades and held them in his left hand. Rising slowly, he squared his chest with the target, focused not on the bull's-eye but the entire area. He wasn't accurate enough to hit the bull's-eye, and he'd never needed to have such precision in real life. There were several areas of the body where a stab wound proved fatal. That's where Ivanov focused his energy. Today was simply practice to keep his eye sharp.

He grasped one knife in his right hand, holding it in the middle, at the balance point, raising his right arm over his shoulder. The arm flashed forward. The sunlight winked off the blade as it sailed to the target. *Thunk*. On the paper. He threw another. *Thunk*. To the right of the first. Another. *Thunk*. Below the second. All six knives closed the distance, the last three as rapidly as Ivanov could throw, and when the last blade left his hand, he was breathless.

Bent with hands on his knees, he examined the target. At twenty yards, it was a good grouping and he felt a muted sense of pride. The impacts were good, but they could always be better. He straightened and had taken one step toward the target when he heard the rumble of a car engine behind him.

He turned. The off-road Mercedes stopped next to a tree. The driver did not get out. The passenger wore a suit, which he brushed at as soon as his dress shoes landed on the dirt ground. He donned a pair of black sunglasses and walked toward Ivanov.

No more practice.

Time for work.

"Yuri Gregorovitch," the man said.

"Yes."

"You are required. Come with us."

Ivanov did not ask permission to collect his knives, and the Kremlin representative knew better than to tell him to leave them. All six knifes found their place in a six-pack carrier attached to a belt. Ivanov rolled the belt into a cylinder and held it in his big left hand.

He boarded the vehicle with the Kremlin rep. His

country needed him again. This was his life, and he did not mind. He was aware of The Hawk's mission overseas, and figured his old friend needed him, and his knives, once again.

Arkady waited for Yuri Ivanov to clear customs. Ivanov carried a black briefcase and matching tote bag. He stood two full inches taller than Arkady, who had to look up to meet the Cossack's eyes.

"Any more bags?"

"This is all."

Arkady turned and started walking. Ivanov fell in step beside him. Arkady said nothing during the drive off the airport property in the rented Lincoln. The Lincoln wasn't as nice as the Mercedes motorcars he was used to in Russia. He also did not like driving and wished the mission budget had included a driver. Such was life. One had to improvise when working in the field, and Arkady was not one to complain openly. Working for the Motherland often demanded sacrifices. He was happy to oblige.

Once they hit the freeway, staying in the slow lane since Arkady was still getting used to the American driving style, the Hawk finally spoke.

"What did they tell you in Moscow, Yuri?"

"That you needed me."

"Nothing of the mission?"

"Nothing of the mission."

"You have a simple task. I need you to deal with any troublemakers who might get in our way."

Ivanov said nothing.

"And don't," Arkady added, "use your knives unless you must."

"Are you expecting trouble?"

"Anything can happen in the next few days. The ship we need to transport the weapon back to Moscow is almost here. Cavallos is taking care of his responsibilities, which includes acquiring a cargo helicopter for his wife to fly. Once I get a close look at Trent's weapon, I'll know better how we're going to take it away. So, yes, Yuri, I am expecting trouble. I'm just not sure what form it will take."

The big Cossack only grunted in reply.

Chapter Twenty-Seven

Trent and Colleen sat at the outdoor café near the office. Colleen had her tablet computer on the table and scrolled through her notes as she and her father talked. The other outdoor tables were full and so was the street, but they didn't need to raise their voices over the extra noise.

"Higgins is already at the house preparing the meal," she said. "Are the engineers coming?"

"Jake Harvey and Frank Kellogg will be there," Trent said. He ate a few bites of Cobb salad.

"What about Pete Kenny?"

"Kid's school play or something, wasn't going to cancel for anything."

Colleen cut her salmon fillet with her fork and swallowed a piece. She didn't know Pete Kenny well, but everybody in the company knew the priority he placed on his family. After her musings the previous evening, she figured he was the smartest person she knew.

"Do you expect to close the sale tonight?" she said.

"We still need to do a demonstration," Trent said, "but if he agrees to that, I think we're home free. Arkady has a big interest in trains, so we'll spend some time with those."

"Oh, wow," she said. "You two will be in the basement for hours."

"I hope that's all it takes and at the end I have his signature on a piece of paper."

Colleen looked up as a dark-haired woman approached the table. Trent watched her, too.

"Pardon me," Nina said, stopping a foot or two from the table, "but I'm Sylvia Lockridge. I'm a freelance journalist and I want to do a story on you, Mr. Trent."

"Now is not a good time."

"Of course, not now. I'm just here to see if we could schedule a meeting."

Colleen said, "How did you hear about my father, Ms. Lockridge?"

"Everybody in D.C. knows who your father is, Ms. Trent." Nina pulled over a stray chair and sat. The Trents shifted a little away from her. "They're also buzzing about laser weapons."

"Our work is classified," Trent said.

"The basics are all over the Internet, Mr. Trent, especially after the Pentagon signed with Hess Laboratories. You know that as well as I do. We just want a profile of the people bringing direct energy technology to reality."

"You should speak with Mr. Hess instead."

"It might be good for business, Dad."

"Not now."

"Won't take more than thirty minutes," Nina said. "Short interview. File photo. Won't disturb you at all."

"Now is not a good time," Trent said again.

Nina took a business card from her purse. She placed the card on the table and slid it to Trent. "If you change your mind, I'm at the DoubleTree till next Thursday."

Colleen watched the dark-haired woman depart. She turned to her father. "Might have been nice."

"We need to finish this deal first. Once that's done, we can see if she's still in town."

"It would give us a chance to talk about other applications of the technology," she said. "Maybe we can generate investment interest."

Her father's eyes flashed anger. "Not *now*, Colleen."

She let out a sigh and watched traffic on the street. There was no getting through to him. Her father looked down at her fish and stopped talking. He said very little for the rest of the meal, and nothing at all on the ride back to the office.

She didn't try to talk to him either.

Trent drove with his hands tight on the steering wheel.

This time *they* wanted to infiltrate his campus. Maybe destroy the 680c and the collected research and development material.

But if he wouldn't let them in, would they try another avenue?

He'd have to discuss the woman's appearance with Arkady when the two of them had a private moment.

Trent slowed, pulling into the driveway and up to the guard shack. The guard pressed a button on his panel, and the main gate swung open. The guard smiled and waved at Colleen. Trent drove through.

Nina sat in the Jag, which she'd parked down the block from the café.

Traffic streamed by as she sat and thought about the encounter.

She wasn't happy, but at least she'd registered her face in their minds. Now what? Plan B, of course.

That meant going to the daughter to tell her everything. She read the daughter's face very well. She wanted a profile for some reason. There was something in it for her. Nina had to find out what and convince her to keep working on her old man.

Trent had said no because the Hawk had his claws in Trent's neck. Must have spun a heck of a yarn about the attempted theft, and Nina wondered if Arkady hadn't orchestrated the whole thing. Such a plan was right up his alley, even working with an enemy of Russia to get it done, but she eliminated the idea once she realized not even John Blaze would have been silly enough to take the deal.

No, somebody else had sent Blaze. The US government was the next most obvious suspect. Trent probably figured that as well, helped along with suggestions from Arkady. So, yeah, he was worried the US would try again. He thought that she was the next attempt at infiltrating, sabotage, whatever.

She started the motor and drove away to find out where Colleen Trent lived.

Arkady had had his doubts about whether or not Ivanov could fit into a proper suit, but the Moscow tailor had done well and the navy blue double-breasted fit the big Cossack just fine. Arkady wore his usual black suit with a white shirt and thin tie, and he held a bottle of wine. Some customs were universal to every culture. Even in Russia, one didn't show up empty-handed.

Arkady knocked on the door of Trent's home. It wasn't as fancy as he had expected. Two-story, small front yard, mixed within a gated community of other homes, some of which were much larger. Perhaps not all capitalists were material gluttons.

A young woman in a strapless red party dress answered and Arkady blinked. Even with the extra weight in her hips, she wore the dress well.

"Hi, I'm Colleen Trent," the woman said. "You must be Alexander. Come in."

The Russians entered the front hall. Inside it was very warm. Delicious smells from the kitchen and voices from the back patio filtered their way. Arkady introduced Ivanov but told her he didn't speak English, which wasn't true at all. He translated her greeting to the big man and Ivanov shook her hand.

"Right this way, drinks on the patio."

Chapter Twenty-Eight

At least they didn't look creepy.

As Colleen Trent led them through the house, self-conscious of how tight her outfit was around the middle, she wondered what else she had expected. Horns? Drooling? They looked like perfectly normal individuals, albeit strangers to her country. If she were visiting Moscow, somebody would have to translate for her, too.

Colleen pushed open the patio doors and announced the new arrivals.

Trent and the two engineers rose from the patio table, which contained an assortment of appetizers. The backyard was larger than the front and had a small gazebo on one side, a greenhouse on the other, and in between some well-maintained grass.

"Alexander," Trent said, after shaking hands with the Russians, "these are two of my top engineers, who probably know more about direct energy than I do. Jake Kenny and Frank Kellogg."

More greetings all around. The engineers weren't very tall, and Kellogg wore glasses. They both were drinking

Cokes. Trent held a half-full martini. They all sat while
Trent fetched drinks: fresh coffee for Arkady and a double
portion of Stoli vodka for Ivanov. Both expressed their
appreciation as Trent rejoined the table. Colleen saw from
the gleam in Arkady's eye that he was pleased to see Trent
remember his preference.

Ivanov said something in Russian. Arkady laughed and
then translated.

"Yuri wants to know where your cowboy boots are."

Trent and the engineers laughed, too. Colleen only
smiled. She'd heard so many cowboy jokes she could
choke on them.

"We're in *real* Texas, not movie Texas," Trent said.
"Two different things."

Ivanov thought that was funny and then, via Arkady,
said he wanted to bring a pair home with him. Trent said
he'd take care of that personally. Colleen knew he'd direct
her to make the purchase. That was fine. It would give her
an excuse to get out of the office for a day or two. The
Russians might not be "creepy", per se, but she didn't like
them. She didn't like her father making this deal, either.
The further away she could get, the better.

They spoke of the weather, family, even hunting. Ivanov turned
out to be an enthusiastic deer hunter. Colleen sat and
listened instead of participating. This was her father's
deal. She'd let him take the lead. If he needed her input,
he would ask for it.

"We have deer in the hills around here," Trent told Ivanov, Arkady translated.

Ivanov responded, and Arkady said to Trent, "Ever
shoot one?"

"I couldn't do that. They haven't done anything to

me. The only deer I ever wanted to shoot nearly wrecked my car."

"How?"

"I was leaving for work early one morning in my little Mercedes convertible, going down the road to the gate, and this big buck leaped right out of the bushes. All I saw was this flash of a head in my lights. I swerved and he slammed into the car, took my side mirror clean off, and when I looked in the rear-view mirror, he was doing a 360 spin on the pavement. I wanted to shoot him for sure, especially when I saw how much it would cost to fix the car."

Arkady translated for Ivanov, who then asked a question.

"What happened to the deer?" Arkady said.

"I drove back to try and find him, but he was gone. Walked it off, I guess." Trent laughed. "Must have had a tough hide."

The chef texted that he was ready to serve dinner. Trent led everybody into the dining room. Arkady told Trent that he couldn't wait to see the train set.

"*Sets*, Alexander. Plural. I have three of them."

The group left the table. Colleen and the engineers made sure to let Trent and the Russians lead the way.

More general conversation accompanied dinner, Arkady telling sto-ries about growing up in Russia, Trent about Texas, and the commonality of their stories impressed Colleen for some reason. Worlds apart yet similar lives. Or maybe everybody was similar, she decided, and we only think we're different, and maybe we'd get along better if we found those commonalities instead of reasons to see each other as different. Nobody at the table mentioned politics or government, which Colleen appreciated. Jake and Frank, the two engineers, were her age and, like her, had been teenagers when the Berlin Wall had come down. But her father and Arkady could both remember the day the wall had gone up. Neither thought they'd see the day when it came down, but Colleen had the distinct impression, based on the edge in Arkaday's voice, that he hadn't been particularly pleased.

The party faded after dessert, where the talk finally turned to technical and business matters, and Jake and Frank chimed in with tidbits about the 680c and related subjects. Arkady focused on how they saw future development and how many weapons Trent could deliver per year. That part made Colleen nervous. If they didn't have enough money to keep the company open more than two months, they certainly had no way to afford a major manufacturing effort, but her father, with complete confidence, promised units could be delivered without trouble.

That part Colleen didn't like for more than financial reasons. It meant the Russians had plans for those weapons. Her anxiety about the deal flooded back, but she pushed it away.

When the chef's staff cleared the dishes, the engineers departed, and Ivanov went outside to smoke.

Colleen poured another glass of wine as her father and Arkady ventured into the basement. She'd needed all the fortification available.

"Oh, wow, this is tremendous."

Theodore Stanton Trent shut the basement door. Before them lay his private worlds, ones he'd created. He swelled with pride. Nobody had told him how to build these worlds, budget was not limited, and he alone controlled what happened. The train sets provided the escape he needed from the stress of running his company.

The three train sets sat atop large tables. The railroad

tracks weaved through decorated mountain passes, small towns and other scenery. One of the train sets circled a moonscape, complete with space stations and astronauts.

Arkady raised an eyebrow.

"When we colonize the moon, we may need trains," Trent said with a grin. "I saw this kit in a magazine once and had to have it. Took me a year to acquire all the individual pieces. I hand-assembled and painted everything."

Arkady examined the mountain set that had the small town. Homes, filling stations, even a drive-in movie theater, the miniature screen playing a recent DVD release, a cable leading from the back of the miniature screen to a compact DVD player concealed within the closest mountain. Trent had staged an accident at one intersection. The miniature model cars and people were painted in bright colors.

Trent fiddled with switches, and the set sparked to life. The model town lit up. The train rumbled along the tracks, passing through tunnels and along the mountains and through the town.

Arkady beamed. Trent examined his face. This was not the Arkady he had met in Monaco. This Arkady wasn't the ice-cold Russian government representative. This version of Arkady was somebody Trent could call friend.

"This is terrific," the Russian said, mesmerized by the moving train.

The third table showed a train circling an international airport, which Trent explained was a work in progress. He wanted to duplicate the Corpus Christi airport, and Arkady pointed out landmarks he had seen firsthand upon landing—more exquisite attention to detail.

Trent let Arkady examine the trains for a while. His normally stoic face had melted in more ways than one.

He looked like a kid at Christmas. Trent took out the business card the dark-haired reporter had given him. He'd placed it in his shirt pocket before the guests had arrived. He returned the card to his pocket. Now was not the time to think about the woman. But when (not if) the Russian deal closed, he'd have a lot to tell the media, and it didn't hurt to have a contact who might help deliver his message.

Unless she truly was a spy. Maybe he'd see what Arkady could dig up. Worth a try.

Chapter Twenty-Nine

Once Colleen and Chef Higgins had left and Trent was alone with Arkady and Ivanov, they sat in the living room with a fresh round of drinks. Trent said, "I've been approached by somebody else."

Arkady froze with his coffee mug an inch from his mouth. "Another buyer?"

"No, a reporter." Trent explained the lunch encounter and passed Arkady the woman's business card.

Arkady put the mug down to examine the card. His stoic expression had returned. He was all business once again. The resurrection of the Ice Man didn't surprise Trent at all. This was his normal state. It took a lot to break the Russian from that state.

"What did you tell her?"

"I refused the offer. After Monaco, I couldn't be sure she wasn't another thief."

Arkady updated Ivanov, who only nodded. Arkady put the card in his pocket.

"We'll check her out," the Russian said. "She could be exactly what she claims."

"Or not."

"Yes, quite possible."

"If she is legitimate, I think I should talk to her. Once our deal is done."

"You want to show off to everybody who rejected you?"

"Something like that," Trent admitted. "I'd like to let everybody know that Trent Defense is still in business, and on the cutting edge of defense designs."

Arkady only nodded and picked up his coffee mug.

"Where's the other fellow who was with you at the hotel?" Trent asked.

"Oh, he's back home," Arkady said. "That's why I had to bring Yuri." Arkady held his mug in his left hand and retrieved the reporter's business card with his right. He looked at it again. "Theo, if your government wanted to stop our deal, they certainly have more direct ways. Especially on your home soil."

"You think I'm overreacting?"

"Don't jump to conclusions. It could be nothing. What did she look like?"

"Very striking," Trent said, and added to the description. "She won't be hard to spot. Or you could visit her hotel room. She wrote it on the back."

"I see it here." He put the card away again. Trent saw something in Arkady's eyes. Wheels spinning. The reporter had stirred something within the Ice Man. Was that good or bad?

The Russian said, "When do we get to see this weapon of yours in action?"

"I thought you'd never ask." Trent smiled.

Arkady handed the business card to Ivanov before he started the Lincoln. Driving away, he said, "Our first troublemaker."

"Second."

Have I already forgotten Blaze? "Right."

Arkady steered down the hill, following the twisting road.

"Watch out for deer."

Arkady slowed the car. "Go to the hotel first thing tomorrow," he said. "I want an ID on the woman before lunch."

"Okay."

The Russians left the gated community without incident.

Nina awoke alone in a quiet room. She had to admit, if only to herself, that her nightmares had increased since seeing Alexander Arkady, but the previous night had been mercifully free of disruptions. Probably because she took a sleeping pill with a shot of Jack Daniels to make sure she conked out.

The dreams were always the same. She was in a room staring at a man half covered by shadows. They didn't speak, but they didn't have to. She knew exactly who she faced.

Nina tossed off the covers, showered and dressed, and went to the hotel restaurant for breakfast. Dane had telephoned the previous night to report all was well. Nina had been pleased to speak with him while totally sober. If he'd noticed, he kept the observation to himself.

After breakfast she pulled on a jacket, tucked her Smith & Wesson M&P Shield 9-millimeter behind her back and went out through the lobby to the garage. She wanted to watch Trent's campus for when Colleen left for lunch. From their first encounter she'd learned that Trent's daughter drove a red Volkswagen. Nina planned to intercept her at lunch once again or, failing that, follow her home, and talk to her one on one about what was happening. She seemed smart. Daughters know their fathers; daughters know when their fathers were in a bad place. Hopefully Nina wouldn't have to explain too much.

Nina did not notice the big Cossack who fell in step behind her.

Very striking, Trent had said.

But he had no idea of whom he was talking about.

Ivanov sat in the lobby, near a television showing the morning news. Other guests clustered around him paid no mind as he divided his attention between the TV and *USA Today*. He scanned the lobby periodically with the woman's description in mind.

When he saw a tall, dark-haired woman in jeans and a tight-fitting T-shirt exit the restaurant, his stomach lurched. Not because she looked good, but because she had a face he'd never forget.

He followed her out to the garage, where she climbed into a Jaguar F-Type. The throaty start of the engine filled the space. Ivanov ran to his car and turned over the motor, speeding after her. He remained a discreet distance behind as he trailed her through town.

He wanted to call Arkady right away, but the Hawk had reminded him that the local cops could pull him over if they saw him on a cell, so he kept the Jag in sight. Ivanov had to pull over for extended periods as the Jag climbed into the hills, but soon recognized the area. Leaving the rental under a tree off the road, he set out through the grass, taking the incline slowly, with eyes alert for the woman's convertible.

Presently he spotted the car parked on the side of the road, but the woman wasn't nearby.

He stayed low in the grass and scanned the distance. Still nothing. He hiked down the slope, across the road, and knelt down in the grass on that side. Thorns poked through his socks, digging irritably into his skin. Only the breeze made its presence known. Then he saw her, lying on her stomach, peering at the Trent campus through binoculars.

Strapped around Ivanov's wait were his throwing knives, each perfectly balanced and razor sharp. Getting them through US Customs required using the X-ray proof bottom of his suitcase, which meant there wasn't enough room for his preferred six knives. He only had four. The knives rode in solid polymer sheaths. He couldn't use leather holders, because the blades risked cutting through. Four knives, two under each arm, and he drew one from under his right. Holding the weapon close, he started forward…and stepped on a twig.

The snap might as well have been a cannon shot. The woman swung a look over her shoulder and spat a curse. Ivanov threw the blade anyway. It whispered through the air, closing the space between, as the woman rolled away. The knife buried itself in the ground where she had lain.

Ivanov dropped and rolled as the woman fired a pistol, a blind shot that went wide. She ran. Ivanov aimed ahead of her and threw another knife that thwacked into a tree. The woman ducked behind the trunk, exposing herself just enough to fire again, but now Ivanov wasn't where he'd been. He crawled up the slope, the grass swishing as he plowed through, circling around her position. He pulled a knife from under his left arm and peeked through the grass. The woman hid behind the tree, most of her body exposed. He rose, bringing his arm back, and was halfway through the throw when the woman turned and fired. As the knife left his hand, Ivanov felt the bullet tear a gash in his wrist. He yelped, dropping to cover. The woman pounded up the slope.

Clutching his wrist, Ivanov followed, the two figures cutting through the grass at a frantic pace. She stayed focused and did not turn to shoot. She angled toward the road. Using his other hand, Ivanov drew his last knife. He stopped. Raised the blade. The woman broke clear of the grass. She fired twice in his general direction, both shots missing. He picked out a spot ahead of her and threw. Sun glinted off the blade as it closed in, but she executed a quick somersault underneath and the knife sailed above her. When she regained her feet, she flashed him a smile.

"Nice try, Yuri!" She raised her gun. He hit the ground. She laughed instead of firing. When Ivanov looked up, she was running for her car.

He stayed low and took out his phone. An ID by lunch. Mission accomplished. He dialed Arkady.

"What is it?"

"That woman," the Cossack said. "Not just a trouble-maker."

"Who is it, Yuri?"

"It's *Nina the Bitch*!"

"Oh, no," Arkady said.

Chapter Thirty

Nina laughed as she powered the Jag down the road.

Yuri Gregorovitch Ivanov. Good with a knife, but not good against a target who knew him. And she knew him well.

She and Dane had guessed correctly. The Russians were not only still dealing with Trent, they'd brought muscle. Nobody brings assassins to a defense deal. Arkady was here for something more sinister.

She steered for town, slowing to the speed limit as she crossed the boundary. She needed to tell Steve, but first needed a new hotel. Ivanov had certainly picked up her trail there, and her sloppiness had almost cost her bigtime. She should have been watching but was too distracted by her own issues. Abandoning the current hotel meant she couldn't return for her stuff. Yuri would report, and there'd be no escaping the agents Arkady spread across the property.

So...no hotel. No clothes. That meant she now had an excuse to go shopping.

The day wasn't a total waste after all.

Arkady hung up after Ivanov's call and began pacing his room. He mashed his teeth angrily. He might have convinced Trent that the US government was behind his trouble, but the truth was far worse. Nina Talikova. *Nina the Bitch.* The woman who had frustrated him time and time again.

If she was here, so was Steve Dane.

Were they connected with the attempted theft? And where *was* Steve Dane? If he wasn't in Texas, it could only mean...

Arkady quickly dialed another number.

Cavallos answered.

"Yes, Alexander?"

"We have a new problem. I need you to look for a man. I'll send you details. Shoot him on sight."

"We're spread thin already," Cavallos said.

"Do not let him get in your way. Do not let him stop you. He *will* try."

"Who is this man?"

Arkady told him.

"Oh, *him*," Cavallos said. "Will his woman be with him?"

"She's *here*."

"Thank you for the tip. We'll be watching."

"We are almost done, Marco. Smash him like a bug and get back here."

Dane's plane landed in Miami where it was sunny and hot. But that wasn't his final destination. Right after arriving he boarded a smaller passenger plane with ten other people for another trip 135 miles north to Vera Beach. That smaller Florida community had only a municipal airport that couldn't handle the jumbo jets landing at Miami International. The vents in the cramped plane piped in warm air and Dane kept one of those vents aimed at his neck. The second leg did not last long and soon he was reunited with both Todd McConn and his luggage.

They shook hands and McConn took Dane to his rental car. With the luggage stowed in the trunk, McConn took over driving detail. The air conditioner filled the cabin with cool air.

"What have you learned so far?" Dane said.

"The Hess plant is a few miles outside of town, and a major employer in this place," McConn said. "I rented a chopper for tomorrow. We can fly over and take some pictures."

"Google Earth is no good this time?"

"I'm sure it is, but I also know you'd want the latest pictures. The Earth map is already outdated. They added a new wing recently."

McConn pulled into a Red Roof Inn and told Dane they had adjoining rooms. The inn was two stories, shaped like a V, with white outer walls and a slanted red roof.

"King bed and high-def television," McConn said as they exited the car.

Dane hefted his bags from the trunk. "You plan on watching TV?"

"We can keep it on in the background. The Jets will look great in HD."

The hotel was indeed clean and comfortable and they spent an hour in McConn's room going over his bag of tricks.

"Got a good digital camera for tomorrow," McConn said as he showed Dane the items in a case.

Dane opened the leather case and examined the Canon PowerShot SX170 in black. He'd used similar cameras in the past and felt confident that the pictures would show the detail he wanted. He nodded his approval.

"Some weapons, HK UMPs, just in case. You brought your .45?"

"Yup," Dane said.

"Okay. I have ammo for it. This you'll like. Genuine Homeland Security identification. All we gotta do is put your picture on this blank one."

Dane examined the whole card with its red border, the DHS logo emblazoned in the upper-left corner.

"Got a camera for that?" Dane said.

"We can use one of those little photo booths at the mall. You know, the ones the teenage girls like."

"Make sure we kick them out first."

"Suit yourself." McConn laughed. "That's all except the standard com unit."

"Let's get my picture squared away. These IDs give me ideas."

At the mall, they found the photo kiosk near the food court, empty, so there was no need to shoo away giggling teenage girls. There was, however, sticker shock, as Dane had to feed the machine $20 for three pictures. Cheaper to take a selfie, but Homeland IDs didn't use those.

He sat in the booth with the curtain closed and faced the camera in the wall before him. The flash went off three times. The machine spit out three small pictures of Dane's dour mug, the expression designed to make him look like a typical federal time-card puncher. Back at the inn, Mc-Conn placed the best of the three pictures in the box on the blank ID, then wrapped a laminate shield around the card by hand. The card fit snugly in the accompanying leather wallet with the gold badge.

"There, you're officially back in Uncle Sam's employ," McConn said.

"After all I've done to get away from it?"

"You should consider it an honor, sir."

"When do I get to start skipping work but still get paid because the union is so powerful, and I can't be fired?"

"What time is it now?"

Dane feigned a punch and McConn laughed.

They went to the restaurant across the street, Mimi's Café, for dinner. A back booth was available near a partially curtained window.

"I like this gig," McConn said, stirring sugar into his iced tea. "Much better than Colombia."

"Any word from Dev?"

"He was up and around when I left, no long-term effects, thankfully."

Dinner was standard fare, a pork chop and potato for Dane while McConn ordered a burger. They skipped dessert and went back to the hotel.

Dane telephoned Nina and they updated each other. Dane noted that she wasn't drunk, which surprised him. Maybe she'd finally noticed the same thing he had, that she was hitting the sauce way too hard.

Chapter Thirty-One

The next day, McConn flew the rented helicopter at 2,000 feet above the city, on a heading for the green countryside east. He kept the 60 highway off to the right side, Dane's side, the whole way.

As they came abreast of Hess Laboratories just beyond the 95 freeway, Dane poked the Canon out through a small side window and snapped pictures in quick succession. McConn continued east for another hour and then turned back, following the same course. Dane captured more photos. Presently they landed, checked in the helicopter with the flight company and returned to the hotel.

They examined the images over lunch in Dane's room.

Hess Laboratories sat a few miles off the 95 and 60, surrounded by open country. Cell towers and a small electrical substation sat nearby, the complex itself a series of buildings on a campus that stretched about three miles east to west.

"Where might the DEW work be happening?" McConn said.

"See that building with the armed guards?"

Dane zoomed in on the spot.

"There they are," McConn said. "Probably won't see that on Google."

"Odd that they don't test outdoors like Trent does."

"Probably environmental reasons. Regulations here are pretty tight." McConn retrieved a notebook from the tote bag. "I did some prelim research on the people involved, too."

He flipped a few pages.

"Mike Watt is the lead engineer. Head of security is Tom Vu."

"Got any pics?"

"No, but I figured we'd meet them when we make our visit. DHS will want to see their setup since they won that contract."

After lunch they drove to a nearby park so Dane could smoke a cigar, as the motel had a no-smoking policy. They sat on top of a picnic table. The grass below the table was brown in patches. Nearby, a woman tossed a Frisbee to her dog, who caught it each time and brought it back to her.

"Any idea where Cavallos might be?" McConn said.

"Oh, he's around. I don't think he or his wife will do the recon themselves."

"He's brought in more people?"

"It's too much to try with only two people. Cavallos will be holed up sorting information and planning."

"And we have no idea when they'll strike?"

"Could be tonight."

"Could be right now."

"We should just forget it then and watch football tonight."

"That's not why I got the TVs," McConn said.

"My gut tells me we still have some time, only not

much. Our best bet, after we get a look at the layout, is to set up our own recon and wait."

"I can get some night-vision gear."

"You mean you forgot that?"

"Can't think of everything."

"Not when you're too busy thinking about sitting on your ass and watching big TVs."

Dane smoked quietly. After a while, they returned to the hotel and Dane called Nina.

"We have a serious problem," Nina said.

"Run out of vodka?"

"No." Dane waited for a sharper reply than that, but she offered none. "Arkady brought in more help," she continued. "Fellow named Ivanov." She described the knife attack.

"If I'd known you'd end up at a reunion," Dane said, "I'd have stuck around."

"Watch your back. Arkady will know you're never too far away but if he thinks we're operating on separate ends of this case, he'll guess where you are."

"Don't worry, I won't leave the hotel. I got a huge TV here."

McConn stopped at the gate in front of Hess Laboratories. He extended his DHS ID as a young guard with a squawking radio on his belt came over to the window. He silenced the radio and took McConn and Dane's IDs. A second guard, who remained in the shack near the gate, watched the car.

The young guard examined the ID cards with a frown.

"We're not expecting you, sir."

"Right. If you knew, this wouldn't be a surprise."

The guard brought both IDs to the other guard, who also examined them. The second guard approached the car.

"You caught us with nobody available to meet you," he told McConn. "Big meeting inside today. Go check in at the reception desk, but you'll have to wait a bit."

"That's fine." McConn took back the ID cards. He drove through and followed the access road to the front parking lot. The receptionist noted the names on their IDs, and they sat in the lobby to wait. The lobby was clean and quiet, gray tiled floor and gray walls. Glass doors divided the lobby from the heart of the offices.

"Not even any outdated magazines to read," McConn said.

"Play Candy Crush on your phone like everybody else."

Presently a man in a blue suit, bald with white hair around his ears and a matching mustache, crossed the lobby to them. Dane and McConn stood up.

Mark Hess introduced himself and apologized for the delay. "We've already had some Homeland guys come through here," he said.

"We're from the local office," Dane said. "More routine, I'm afraid. Gotta be done."

Hess let out a sigh. "Let's get started then. We have top-notch security here."

Dane didn't sense any enthusiasm from Hess, but why would he? Whatever the day's agenda contained, Dane and McConn had derailed. *It's for your own good, buddy.* They moved outside and Hess gave an overview of the campus, how many buildings, employees. He pointed out that the armed guards were private contractors.

"Why not federal cops?" McConn said.

"Defense Department won't supply them. Budget cuts."

Now it was Dane's turn to not be happy. How did the United States plan to protect companies like Hess where classified work was conducted on taxpayer funding when they didn't have the resources to make sure people like Arkady access the building? Private contractors, with their solid military backgrounds, were probably better suited to the detail than federal cops, he had to admit, but the out-sourcing made it seem like the Feds didn't care one way or the other. *Somebody else will do it.*

"How are you fixed for communications?" Dane asked.

"We have land lines, cellular backup and an under-ground generator to keep things going during a power failure."

"So that substation we passed—"

"Is part of the power company. With us out in the boonies like this, they had to put it there."

Hess steered them toward the largest building on the campus. They crossed a wide courtyard of concrete with patches of green grass, benches, a few trees. Security crews drove around in Ford SUVs.

"This is where our directed-energy work is done," Hess said. The guards in front wanted to see their identification. When the guards cleared them, Hess led Dane and McCo-nn into a large open area, almost like a warehouse. Some cubicles sat in one corner, but most of the activity on the cold concrete floor was at a large saucer-shaped "radar dish" mounted atop a Hummer. Engineers hovered around referencing notes on clipboards while technicians fussed with the DEW itself.

"There she is," Hess said. "The prototype anyway. The XM-47."

"No test yard here?" Dane said.

"We test off-site." Hess called over one of the engineers. The thirtysomething man, clipboard tucked under his arm, looked sweaty. "This is Mike Watt, our lead engineer."

Dane and McConn shook hands with Watt. Hess asked

Watt to explain some of the DEW functions, and Watt stuttered every few words, but answered the questions. It wasn't hot in the warehouse, but Watt sweated during the conversation, but made no move to wipe his forehead. When he finished his rundown, Hess dismissed Watt and called over a passing guard. The uniformed man wore a pistol, and Hess introduced him as Tommy Vu, the head of security. Vu described the duties of his men, adding that a full complement of twenty worked day and night. After a few minutes Vu carried on with his work and Hess escorted Dane and McConn back to the lobby.

As they drove away, McConn said, "Blow the substation, the cell towers, the phone lines and that generator he's so proud of, and you can have the run of the place."

"You'd need more than a handful of guys to take on that guard force, though."

"If they have the right experience and aren't soft from all that standing around," McConn said. "Don't give them too much credit."

"What did you think of that Watt fellow?" Dane said.

"He was sweating a lot."

"Seemed awfully nervous."

"Think we should pay him a visit?"

"Won't hurt," Dane said.

Chapter Thirty-Two

Lead engineer Mike Watt lived at the end of a quiet cul-de-sac, and McConn parked across the street from the single-level home. The sun had gone down and evening was well underway. The driveway of Watt's home was empty, but that didn't last long. Watt slowed his Honda as he pulled up and exited the car with a cell phone to his ear. He did not notice Dane and McConn. Watt entered the house.

"How do you want to handle this?"

Dane tapped his lip and looked at the house. "I think—"

Two gunshots cut him off.

Dane and McConn bolted from the car and ran to the house. Dane tried the front door, which was locked. They ran around the front of the house to the fence, hopping over and banging the fence loudly as they climbed. As soon as Dane's feet hit the dirt, an armed man ran across the backyard to the fence on the opposite side. Dane ordered him to stop as he drew the Detonics Scoremaster and sighted down the barrel. The running man fired. Dane and McConn hit the ground as the bullet chunked into the fence behind them, Dane triggering two rounds in reply as the shooter vaulted over the fence. The neighbor's dog started barking.

"We gotta move!" McConn said. They hopped over the fence again and ran back to the rental, speeding away.

"I think that's our answer," McConn said, his hands loose on the wheel. "Shoot the inside man before the strike."

Dane stowed the Detonics under his jacket. "It's going to be a long night," he said.

"Are we going back for our gear?"

"We don't have time to pick up our gear."

McConn steered through traffic while Dane clenched his jaw and right fist. He didn't like being behind the eight ball, and in this case, they were probably further behind than he realized. The attack might be halfway over before they reached the Hess campus, and then what? McConn didn't regularly carry a weapon. Were they going to take on Cavallos and his team with only Dane's pistol?

He hoped Tommy Vu, head of security, and his private contractor force held their own until they arrived. There was still no guarantee of victory, but it might help.

Marco Cavallos spread the hand-drawn map of the Hess plant on the hotel room table. Red and blue circles noted bomb targets. Scribbled notes also dotted the paper.

Roxana stood beside her husband. Two other men, Foster and Lenz, freelancers Cavallos had brought aboard for the job, stood on the other side of the table. Lenz had been the shooter at Mike Watt's house. Cavallos had not liked the report about the two other men arriving as he escaped and figured the new arrivals were the people Arkady had warned him about.

Which meant they were now out of time and the clock was ticking. Luckily Cavallos and his people were well-prepared. The days leading up to the Watt murder had been well spent indeed.

But they couldn't afford to rush. The plan had to be executed carefully as they'd have only one chance to blow up the Hess weapon.

It wasn't a long briefing, since the four had been planning over the previous few days. Roxana would blow the substation with four blocks of C-4. They'd have five minutes to get over the perimeter fence before the generator activated. Foster would take down the phone lines and cell tower. Cavallos and Lenz would take care of the generator, and then link up with Roxana and Foster on the east corner of the campus—near the building housing Hess's DEW and finish the job.

Lenz spoke after Cavallos had finished the review. "The two shooters at Watt's house. What do we do if they show up?"

"We'll deal with them the same way we'll deal with the rest of the Hess security people. What can two more guns possibly do against us? They're coming in cold. We've been here for over a week."

It was bravado Cavallos didn't quite believe, but he needed the two men to believe it. Roxana probably saw through the statement, but she also wasn't going to contradict her husband. He hoped they did believe his words. He didn't want them getting spooked and running away at the last minute. He'd paid them enough that they should stick around, but mercenaries cared as much for their own lives as they did their paychecks. Sometimes one became more important than the other.

"And how will they get onto the property?" Roxana said.

"Or engage us at the end?" Vargas said.

"It's not your problem," Cavallos said. "Let me worry about those two. Just watch your back and we'll be fine. Let's get our gear together and move out."

Two minutes.

Cavallos and Lenz hopped out of the back of the white panel van driven by Roxana and ran off the road into the brush. The van moved on. Cavallos and Lenz, like Foster and Roxana, were clad head to toe in black with black grease paint shading their faces. Armed with M-4 carbines with attached silencers, pistols and grenades, they charged up the rise to their position, where they would wait until the first explosions detonated.

Anything loose on their combat webbing had been taped with black duct tape. Their gear made some noise as they climbed, but not as much as their stomping boots made on impact with the soft ground. Cavallos hadn't expected the ground to be soft, but it was, and they had to deal with it. Luckily there weren't any people, or Hess guards, around to hear them.

Cavallos looked to his left at Lenz. The mercenary kept up with him, his eyes on their final position. They both breathed hard as they powered up the rise.

Cavallos had stated two minutes from van to lookout to make sure they were prepared for when the roving patrol passed by their starting position. They would need the Jeep to bust through the electrified fence. Whoever had designed the fence knew how to do it properly, for maximum effectiveness: there were two fences, both electrified, with a gap in between. The design was a precaution against anybody who might defeat the first fence. What Cavallos wanted to do was crash the Jeep through the barriers. No electrified fence could prevent that.

Lenz let out a cry and toppled forward, hitting the ground with a grunt. Cavallos, after two steps, stopped and turned. Lenz pushed back to his feet. "Rock," he said. He started moving again, passing Cavallos. He wasn't limping or otherwise hurt. He checked his watch. One minute. Cavallos tucked his rifle close to his body and began the climb again.

Chapter Thirty-Three

Presently they took their positions. Clouds in the dark sky, the moon barely visible. Everything around them was dark. They hid in the brush about twenty-five yards from the Hess perimeter, marked by an electrified fence with warning signs in several languages.

A few seconds late, but nothing too terrible.

As their breathing returned to normal and they adjusted to the darkness, Cavallos grew nervous, the cold air unable to dry the sweat on his neck. What if something happened to Roxana before she accomplished her task?

The rumble of a motor reached their ears.

Almost time.

Roxana approached the substation on foot. She walked casually with a weighted pack on her back. There were no guards at the substation. The only security was a padlocked gate. Barbed wire topped the fence, but that was no concern. There was nobody around to see her. She'd left the panel van far behind.

Roxana used a bolt cutter from the pack to snip a length of the chain-link fence. She had to press hard on the handles before the razor-sharp blades of the bolt cutters snapped the link. She cut two extra links to make sure she had the room. She had a compact body, but she was carrying a lot of gear. She didn't want that getting stuck.

She squeezed through the gap, the pack catching momentarily. She stopped, taking a deep breath to remain calm. A strap had caught. She pulled free. Moving away from the fence, she removed the pack and held it close.

The racks of coils and transformers hummed a few feet above her, but Roxana's attention was on the four metal cabinets on a flat concrete slab that kept the works going. At each cabinet, she placed a block of C-4 explosive with a remote-activated blasting cap. With the C-4 in place, she slipped back through the fence, and ran about 100 yards to take cover behind a pair of trees growing out of the ground in a V shape. A quick check of her watch showed her two minutes behind schedule. Her husband would not like that. Oops. She pulled a detonator from her utility belt and pressed the button. The blast shook the ground even at her distance, and the flames lit up the night in a brief flare that faded quickly. Fire consumed what remained of the substation, the fallen racks of coils and transformers a flaming pile of junk.

She left the tree and broke into another sprint for the Hess campus not too far away.

Cavallos certainly bristled at the two-minute delay, and not only because his wife was behind schedule. He feared she'd been intercepted. But when the bomb finally lit the sky with a bright flash, he forgot his concern.

At the same moment, the headlights of the patrol Jeep appeared over a rise to the left, the engine louder now, the driver stomping the brakes as orange flame lit the night.

No words passed between Cavallos and Lenz. They rose slightly, M-4s at their shoulders. Silenced shots popped in rapid succession, the windshield caving, the guards yelling as 5.56mm slugs chewed through their flesh.

Cavallos took the lead, Lenz behind him, as they double-timed to the Jeep. Cavallos hauled out the driver and let his body crash to the ground. Lenz did the same and jumped into the passenger seat as Cavallos put the Jeep in gear. He gunned the engine, turning right, away from the fence, long enough to get some distance. He wrenched the wheel left, the pedal all the way down now as the Jeep rushed headlong toward the chain-link.

The vehicle crashed through, sparks flying. They were the only light in an otherwise dark countryside.

The lights around the campus were out. Darkness reigned. Cavallos and Lenz left the Jeep and ran through the property using their night-vision goggles, the campus bathed in a strange green glow through the eyepieces.

The generator sat a few feet underground, accessed by recessed steps near the center of the campus. As Cavallos and Lenz approached, two armed guards challenged them with raised rifles. The silenced M-4s spat slugs into the two guards before either could fire or shout.

Lenz dropped to one knee as Cavallos relieved one of the dead men of the generator door key.

Two more explosions flashed in the distance. The cell towers, gone blooey.

The key turned in the lock, and Cavallos entered the generator room. Two power units sat in the small space. A block of C-4 at each, the remote blasting caps primed, and Cavallos climbed back to the surface. He and Lenz ran for cover as shouts from organizing guards came their way. The belowground blast, which created a dusty crater where the steps had been, drowned out the shouts. Cavallos and Lenz broke cover and headed for the east corner of the campus.

Tommy Vu, the head of security at Hess Laboratories, hadn't planned on his shift's ending this way.

When the lights went out, he'd been behind his desk sorting paperwork. No problem. The power went out once or twice a year. But the rumble of an explosion followed the blackout. Using his Maglite, he went out to the front of the security office.

Two officers sat at a circular desk in front of a row of blank monitors. A radio set rested beside the bank of screens.

"Sounded like a bomb," one of the security men said.

"Agreed," Vu said. He picked up a walkie-talkie from one side of the desk. It worked on the cellular network. He keyed the Talk button. "Anybody see an explosion?"

"It came from the area of the substation," reported another guard. "Flames sky high."

"I want everybody on alert," Vu said. "Full weapons, be ready—"

Two more explosions. The walkie-talkie went dead in Vu's hand.

"Outside!" he shouted, using the Maglite on his belt to lead the way out of the office.

The next explosion was the loudest. The building shook and knocked Vu off his feet. His men helped him up. He didn't need to be told what had blown up. He turned to the man on his left.

"We can't call out. Get in your car and drive to police headquarters. Get them out here."

The security guard nodded and took off running.

"We need to get to the armory," Vu told the other man. The beam from his flashlight led the way.

Chapter Thirty-Four

Roxana neared the Hess complex, approaching from the front. She saw a car peel out of the parking lot and speed down the access road to the main road. She threw her M-4 to her shoulders and opened fire. The silenced weapon clicked as the action cycled and spent casings ejected rapidly from the side. The slugs smashed into the side of the car, windows shattering, the driver letting out a scream as the bullets found their mark. The car careened off the access road, across the grass to the main road, where the tires screeched some more before the vehicle collided with a tree trunk with a horrendous crash. Metal screeched as it twisted with the impact and wrapped around the tree. Roxana reloaded and ran for the fence. She traveled the perimeter, up the rise and dips in the terrain, until she found where Cavallos had breached the fence with the Jeep. She sprinted through the gap.

She stopped near a dark building and peered around the corner, the green glow of her night-vision goggles high-lighting nearby security guards who were toting weapons similar to hers. No expense spared. The Hess guards were passing the building and spreading out on the orders of a squad leader. Four of them. Roxana swung her weapon around the corner. She fired two quick bursts. Two of the guards dropped, crying out. Their compatriots went down and rolled, one yelling for where the shots had come from. Roxana tracked the speaker, fired, missed. He fired back but randomly into the surrounding shadows. Roxana fired again. The salvo punched through the guard's head. The last started to run, shouting for help. Roxana stroked the trigger once more and the shouting stopped. The last guard fell face-first onto the ground. She changed magazines and moved forward, her boots stomping on the dirt.

The night vision offered no peripheral visibility—one of its drawbacks. A shout on her left made Roxana stop and turn. More guards yelled at her. She answered by emptying the magazine, spraying rounds, driving the troops to take cover. She reloaded on the run. Return fire zipped around her but they were firing into the dark. So far, she still had the advantage of being able to see them clearly.

She passed the still-smoking crater where the generator had once stood. The smoke drifted across her face, irritating her nose.

More shouting. She found cover behind a hedge and peeked through an opening. With no coms, Hess's security force communicated verbally. Brief blasts of flashlights marked them. She listened to another squad leader give directions. She poked the muzzle of her weapon through the hedge and let loose two single shots. The leader did not fall, but he rolled for cover, blind return fire snapping through the night.

She broke cover and ran again.

When she reached the east corner, Cavallos, Lenz and Foster were waiting as planned. Her husband asked,

"Have fun?"

"They're scattered and unorganized," she said.

"We're running out of time."

"Let's not waste anymore talking."

Cavallos ran toward the test building.

MCCONN SLOWED at the sight of the wrecked car with the dead man inside. He did not stop. It did not take much examination to determine what had happened.

"Hurry," Dane said. The front building was in complete darkness, and no lights showed anywhere else that he could see from the road.

McConn sped up, stopping at the gate.

"No good government man would crash the gate," he said, hopping out to manually push the gate open, the motor that would have done it automatically making an awful thunk noise as he opened the gate all the way. He jumped back behind the wheel and flashed past the parking lot to the front steps.

Dane and McConn ran up the steps to the front door. Dane tried the handle, but it wouldn't budge. He pounded several times.

"We'll have to hop the fence," Dane said.

"We'll get blasted."

Somebody approached the door. A guard with a weapon. Dane flashed his DHS ID and shouted through the glass. "Homeland Security! We're here to help!"

The guard inside kept his submachine gun at his hip. "Stay back!"

"Tom Vu knows us! Get Tom Vu!"

The guard ran off. Dane turned to McConn. "Maybe jumping the fence isn't a bad idea."

Single shots popped. One-sided firing.

"They're shooting at shadows," McConn said.

The front door opened as a breathless Tom Vu stuck his head out. He glanced at both Dane and McConn, said okay and let them in.

"I sent one of my men for help," Vu said.

"They shot him off the road. We saw the wreck on the way in," Dane said.

"Then we need to handle this ourselves. Let's get you two some weapons."

Presently Dane and McConn, with their issued semi-auto HK MP-5s, joined what remained of Vu's force. They were spread out in a line near the back of the main building.

"They're going for the DEW," Dane explained. "We need to secure the building."

"They've been picking us off," Vu said. "We can't hear them shooting, so they have silencers. Probably night vision. What do you suggest?"

"Divide your men into three groups. We'll converge on the test center on three sides."

"They'll see us coming."

"I saw your SUVs earlier. Round them up so they face the building and turn on the headlights. Extra points if you hit the high beams."

Vu gave the orders. Dane and McConn accompanied him and four other men. They took the lead while the other two squads ran for the SUVs. Dane's team stayed low as they moved across the open area. It was like charging a machine gun nest in the open desert. Nowhere to hide. Moving shadows played tricks on their eyes, but nobody fired.

Dane looked ahead but the darkness never wavered. The moon's glow failed to provide even a fraction of illumination. But then—

"Stop," Dane whispered. "Down."

Behind them, the SUVs drove into position. Headlights popped on and gave the courtyard some light, if only a little, as the beams couldn't cross the entire distance. The light wasn't to help the defenders see but to frustrate the night vision of the enemy.

Right away rapid clicking echoed across the distance. Men started yelling, with single shots cracking in response. Some of the headlights burst as high-velocity slugs tore into them. Muzzle flashes on the left meant one of Vu's teams had started returning fire. The remaining headlights created more shadows around the test building than any visible targets, but Dane ordered the team to shoot that way anyway.

The HKs crackled as the team squeezed off short bursts.

Chapter Thirty-Five

Enemy fire zipped overhead, audibly buzzing. Dane and McConn fired in a synchronized pattern. Left, right, center, the idea being that a steady stream would find a target. Vu's men fired randomly. More headlights winked out and then there was darkness again.

Dane yelled, "Forward!"

He and McConn led the charge, with Vu and his men spreading out behind. One man screamed, then another. Dane leaped ahead and collided with a black-clad figure. He yanked off the man's night-vision gear, and the man kneed Dane in the stomach. He took the blow but didn't fall, slamming his right elbow repeatedly into the man's face as he tried to get his wind back. His next blow faltered, the black-clad man breaking away to strike Dane in the chest.

Dane dropped, rolled away, groaning and sucking air in short gasps. The man reached for his weapon. Dane scrambled back to his feet as McConn stitched six rapid rounds across the shooter's chest.

Dane stood and grabbed the night-vision goggles, still

hurting from the blows, but there was no time to stop and lick wounds. The fight would not wait for him. He adjusted the eyepieces and scanned the area. No other shooters in sight. He zeroed in on the test facility as Vu called for his other teams to rally. One of the windows shattered outward and the snout of a silenced M-4 carbine filled the hole.

"Everybody down!"

As Cavallos and his team reached the test building, he ordered Lenz to take watch outside. Lenz broke off and dropped flat a few yards away. Roxana rigged the entrance with a charge and stepped back. The door blew inward with the blast. Cavallos, his wife, and Foster entered the dark building.

"Foster," Cavallos said, "take a window."

Foster did so while Cavallos and Roxana ran to the vehicle supporting the Hess DEW.

Roxana shed her pack and opened the top. She handed her husband two blocks of C-4.

Cavallos went to the DEW and began placing the charges, one at the front of the vehicle and the other under the gas tank, which was directly beneath the mounted dish.

Roxana, weapon slung, with two more charges in either hand, placed her bombs at the base of a wall on each side of the building.

"They're coming!" Foster said. "They got lights!"

Gunfire crackled outside.

"He only has to hold them a few seconds," Cavallos shouted. He finished wiring the remote blasting cap in place.

"Ready," Roxana said, returning to Cavallos.

"Same," he said.

Then Foster smashed the window. "They got Lenz!" He let a string of rounds go, shifting as he fired.

"Doesn't matter now," Cavallos said. He raised his M-4

and shot Foster in the back. The man screamed, falling forward into the wall before gravity pulled him to the floor, the rifle pinned beneath his body.

Cavallos and Roxana ran out the door where they'd entered. Cavallos held the detonator in his left land.

Some of Vu's men wailed from their wounds. Non-wounded dragged them away from the fusillade coming from the building. Then the shooting stopped. Dane watched the man in the window fall, his scream carrying across the night.

Obviously Cavallos wasn't leaving dead weight or loose ends behind.

And the disposal of the shooter meant only one thing.

"They're gonna blow the building. Get back!"

As the group retreated, Dane spotted two figures running out the side door. Then he tore off the night-vision goggles. The blast inside the building blew out the remaining windows, orange fire whooshing out. The next two blasts folded in the walls. The roof collapsed. Chunks of debris flashed through the air, landing near Dane, McConn and Vu's men. The ground shook and the sound of the explosion hammered eardrums into submission.

Dane stood and shouted at McConn to get Vu's men inside. He went to Lenz's body and helped himself to the full-auto M-4 and ammo.

"You can't go after them alone!" McConn said.

"I'm the only one who can see them!" Dane refitted the night-vision goggles. He ran in the direction the departing figures took, holding the captured M-4 close to his chest.

He ran wide around the burning building, the green glow of the night vision flaring as the sensors picked up the increased light from the flames. He felt the heat, too, especially against the exposed areas of his face and neck.

Any closer, he'd sear skin.

The two figures ahead reached the east fence. One start-ed to climb over. The destruction of the generator meant the fence was no longer electrified.

Dane stopped, took aim and fired. The climbing figure rolled over the side and dropped to the ground, falling flat, scrambling away. The other fired back. The slugs kicked up dirt and flashed by Dane's head. He ran, dropped, rolled. Aimed again. The second figure cleared the fence and land-ed on the other side, Dane's rounds only driving the figure to cover. One of them threw a grenade over the fence. The explosive orb sailed Dane's way, arcing down to land a few yards away. Dane covered his head as the blast tore a crater out of the earth. Shrapnel nicked at his clothes. Dane jumped up and ran in a zigzag to the fence.

He fired through the chain-link, sweeping left to right. The fence shook and rattled as he climbed. His pants ripped on the barbed wire. He rolled over the top and landed hard. Staying flat, he scanned the tree line. No sign of any move-ment. He started forward, running from tree to tree. Still nothing. He broke cover for a tree a few feet ahead.

Somebody stepped around that tree and tossed another grenade in a leisurely underhand pitch.

Dane batted the grenade away with the M-4. It flew off to the right, bouncing off another tree to come right back at him. He rolled away as the blast thundered through the night. His left leg burned as shrapnel tore into the flesh, more bits stinging his neck and cracking the side of the night-vision goggles. The image went out. Dane tossed the goggles aside but adjusting from greenish glow to darkness ruined his sight for the moment. Footsteps pounded away. Dane fired at random, but his slugs con-nected only with trees or brush.

Dane jumped up, grimacing at the pain flaring through his right leg. He hobbled to a tree and leaned against the trunk. He lifted the M-4 to his shoulder but then lowered the muzzle. The shadows held no further threats.

He pushed on anyway until he cleared the tree line. The open field ahead only confirmed that the quarry had slipped away.

Dane sat against a tree and looked at his leg, plucking out two pieces of the grenade, gritting his teeth against the flare of pain that followed before subsiding to a dull throb. The shrapnel hadn't gone deep but sure felt like it had. Grunting, Dane forced himself upright and started the long walk back.

Chapter Thirty-Six

Vu and his remaining men set up a hospital in the front lobby for the wounded. The dead they left outside. Dane sat against a wall as McConn used a first-aid kit to clean and dress Dane's leg wound.

"Bones heal," McConn said, "and chicks dig scars."

"That's the rumor."

Another of Vu's men went for help, and after a while two ambulance crews and a fire truck arrived, the cops not far behind. More fire crews joined the mix and took care of the burning test building. When Hess himself arrived, he examined the scene in shock.

Dane, McConn and Vu gave their statements to police, who eventually talked to the entire security force, too.

They remained there through the night. When the sun came up, Dane and McConn were finally able to leave, their cover intact. Their DHS credentials might fall apart on further scrutiny, but they had served their purpose. Dane and McConn were not detained. Returning to the hotel, Dane took a hot bath, keeping his right leg elevated on the side of the tub. He stared at the wall in a daze for a long time.

Arkady would move against Trent now that his people had destroyed the Hess facility. Dane and McConn had to get back to Texas and fast.

Dane performed an awkward roll out of the tub and lay on the floor to catch his breath. He sat up to dry off and then stood to wipe the water from the floor. As the tub drained, he tied on a robe and stretched out on the bed to call Nina.

"Are you hurt badly?" she said after he finished his update.

"I'll live. Believe me when I tell you I have a score to settle with Mr. Arkady."

"I believe you," Nina said, "and you aren't the only one. Hurry back, darling. I can't do this alone."

"Stay out of sight until I get there."

Nina ended the call and let out a deep breath. At least he was okay.
She'd moved to another hotel without incident and now she looked around the empty room. Forty-eight hours without a drink. Now she felt entitled. Opening the room's small fridge, she selected a small plastic bottle of Stoli vodka. She sat on the bed and drank it down in two swallows. The vitamins burned down her throat and warmed her tummy. Nothing to do now but wait for Steve. She grabbed a second bottle and turned on the television, hoping she could find something to watch.

Even a dumb reality show might fill the void until Dane returned. Anything to keep her mind off—

She drank another swallow of vodka.

Dane crossed into McConn's room. McConn was on the bed, flipping channels with the remote.

"I booked us a flight for Texas tomorrow afternoon,"

Dane said.

"Join up with Nina?"

"And finish this, yes. Get some sleep."

"You're not my boss anymore."

Dane shook his head. Some things never changed, such as McConn's smart mouth. He closed the connecting door and climbed into bed. His leg ached but a pair of Advil tablets dulled the pain enough that he didn't have trouble eventually falling asleep. His subconscious would sort out the problems they faced while he dozed. As he drifted off, he wondered what Nina was doing, and hoped she didn't have any nightmares.

He showered the next morning, replaced the bandages on his leg, dressed and ordered room service, specifying a few extra tea bags with his pot of hot water. When the knock came, he answered, only to freeze at the sight of a man holding a gun.

"Please step back, Mr. Dane," the man said.

Mid-twenties, Dane guessed. He raised his hands and followed directions. The new arrival wore a black suit, which contrasted his pale skin. French accent. At least it wasn't Russian.

The new arrival entered and held the door. Three others followed him inside. Each man was much older than Dane, wrinkled faces, age spots, and various shades of gray hair indicating their elder status.

One of them said to the Frenchman, "Put the gun away and shut the door." The Frenchman slipped the gun under his jacket and stood against the door with his hands cupped in front of him.

"Lower your hands, Mr. Dane."

"American?"

"All three of us," said the old man nearest Dane. "We

come in peace. We also need to talk about Texas."

Dane indicated the table, where two of the men sat. The third sat on the edge of the bed.

Dane leaned against the dresser.

The man on the bed spoke.

"You may refer to me as Number One. My associates are Two and Three."

"Can't count any higher?"

"I see your injuries have not affected your alleged wit," said Number One. "We call ourselves The Trust. All three of us once worked deep within US intelligence. We have, by the way, several mutual friends, Mr. Dane."

"Okay."

"President Cross is one such mutual friend."

"Sure."

"We mean no harm."

"What is this about? You know President Cross, big deal. I worked for the man. Did you?"

"He worked for me."

"This keeps getting better."

"Mr. Dane, I don't have to explain to you the danger the world faces, from a variety of threats and psychopaths who want nothing more than to cause as much chaos as possible.

"The official means of combating these threats are mired in politics, backroom deals, second-guessing and red tape. You know this. My associates and I decided to use our skills and connections to face those threats head-on. We gather information and send freelancers from all walks of life to deal with the problems."

"I'm starting to get the picture," Dane said.

"You met our operative, John Blaze, in Monaco," said Number One. "He was tasked with stealing Mr. Trent's papers before Arkady saw them."

"Thanks for clearing up that plot point, but what does that have to do with me?"

"We knew you were there, you and Miss Talikova, and we assumed rightly that your nature wouldn't allow you to turn away. We have kept an eye on you to see how far you'd get."

"I'm sorry to say it hasn't been very far at all."

"No, but Mr. Hess is a resourceful man. He will bounce back. Arkady destroyed the machine, not the man who made it."

"Does that mean Hess is in danger?"

"Arkady doesn't have the time and even Hess's death wouldn't stop the rebuilding. For better or worse, direct-energy weapons are here to stay."

"What do you want from me?"

"What do you think we want?"

"I know you didn't come here to ask me to stop," Dane said.

"Of course not. We have a gap in our workforce, and I'd like you and Miss Talikova to fill it."

"We do fine on our own. The last time I worked for people like you, it didn't turn out so well."

"We will not assault your autonomy," said the old man. "We want you to finish what you've started. We offer aid, information and payment. In exchange, you become our operative. In the future, we will call you and ask you to do a job. That's the deal."

"Not interested."

"Of course, you aren't."

Dane folded his arms. "I can't wait to see what you say next."

"What do you see when you look in the mirror, Mr.

Dane?"

"A face that's getting older."

"And?"

"If you know as much as you say, I don't have to tell you."

"Indeed. You see your scars every day. You've convinced yourself that a freak accident almost ended your life, and you need to proceed with caution when diving into new dangers. Mr. Dane, what if I told you that helicopter crash was intentional? Somebody sabotaged the machine. Somebody was trying to kill you."

Dane answered only with a blank stare. For once, his mind had gone quiet. The Frenchman could take out his gun and demand a response and Dane still wouldn't have been able to find the words.

"I do not wish to remind you of painful matters," Number One said, "but it's important that I do. Your father was accused of treason. He later shot himself. This is fact, correct?"

Dane nodded stiffly.

"You didn't believe the treason story. You especially didn't appreciate your friends and colleagues suddenly looking on you with suspicion. Like father like son? Could you still be trusted? Is this correct?"

Finally, Dane uttered, "Yes."

"You managed to do a little investigation, but your efforts were frustrated, because it seemed as if your father had done exactly what he was accused of."

Dane nodded.

"And then your helicopter crashed. Did you ever tie the two threads together, Mr. Dane?"

Dane cleared his throat. Resolve returned. He said, "No. I did not."

"You were very close, young man. Very close to learning the truth. Had you not given up, had you not run off on your own, perhaps you might have solved the mystery."

"Perhaps I'd be dead."

"That too."

"Get to the point."

"Mr. Dane, your father was murdered and the same people tried to kill you. When that failed, they tried to discredit you, but your departure ultimately helped them. You were out of the way. They moved forward without further meddling from the Dane family."

"So my father was—"

"Investigating CIA corruption, Mr. Dane."

Dane's shoulders sagged.

"You were trying to find proof of your father's innocence, but you've been looking in the wrong places."

"If I join you, you'll provide the clues I need?"

"Exactly. Change your mind?"

"I think I need a drink."

"Not on the job, Mr. Dane." Number One laughed. "Do we have an agreement?"

"Yes," Dane said. "Assuming I survive Texas, we have an agreement."

"Oh, you'll survive. You have a new reason to."

"What else should I know about Arkady?"

Number One glanced over at Number Three. "That's your cue."

Number Three leaned forward. He had a softer voice than Number One. "Arkady plans to steal Trent's weapon and get it out of the United States via ship. That ship is currently twenty-four hours away from the rendezvous point off the Texas coast. The weapon cannot get on that ship, Mr. Dane."

"How does he plan to move the weapon? He certainly can't drive it."

"Roxana Cavallos is a helicopter pilot," said Number Three. "We assume they will use a cargo chopper."

"Were she and her husband at the Hess place last night?"

"They were."

"Too bad I didn't kill them then."

Number One said, "Perfection eludes all of us, Mr. Dane. We keep trying."

"Who is your source?" Dane said.

"Somebody deep inside the Kremlin," said Number One. "The growing issues with Russia demand a return to, shall we say, the practices of days we thought were long behind us."

"And peace eludes us, too."

"Right you are, but maybe we can prevent another war."

"I have a plane to catch."

"And breakfast waiting," said Number One as he rose. "We made the poor fellow wait outside. Enjoy your meal, Mr. Dane. We were never here."

The Frenchman opened the door, and the three old men left. The door remained open after the Frenchman departed, and the room service waiter wheeled in the cart with breakfast for two. The waiter said it might be a little cold, but Dane didn't mind. He tipped the waiter well and apologized for making him wait in the hallway. After the waiter departed, he went next door to wake up McConn.

Dane told his friend about the meeting as they ate.

"Think they're on the level?"

"They'd better be," Dane said, "or I'll kill all three of them."

"What about your old man?"

Dane sighed. "What about him indeed."

Chapter Thirty-Seven

Dane, in the window seat on the flight to Texas, thought about the three old men as he stared at the blue sky.

Their statements made him cycle back to the days before his departure from the United States. He thought about every name, every face, that his father had contact with (that he also knew of) and examined each person as closely as his mind allowed. He thought about his own investigation, how President Cross had stopped him from shooting a man he claimed had nothing to do with the matter, and anything else his subconscious offered that he had suppressed for so long.

Eventually he came up with a suspect for the helicopter sabotage that had left him scarred for life. The scars he covered to hide the deeper ones within.

Like his father, Dane had been an eager patriot with a desire to serve his country and he'd never believed for one second that his father had lived a lie. His suspect's position in the government, as well as his standing, might prevent him from moving forward without risking prison. Dane was no good to his father's ghost behind bars. And who pulled the strings behind Dane's suspect? How deep did the corruption described by The Trust go?

If the old men could deliver their promised support, Dane would have muscle equal to his suspect's and that of any cronies behind him.

If he could expose the truth, he'd finally have the justice he craved. He might have to modify his approach. To enter shooting might cause more problems than it solved. He might need a little more finesse. He smiled. Alone, he might not have been able to pull it off; with Nina, with McConn and Stone, he could do it.

And his gut told him The Trust was right.

Dane would soon deliver a long overdue reckoning and the idea filled him with new energy and purpose. The enemy had tried to kill the wrong man. They thought Dane running off served their purpose. It hadn't. It only made Dane stronger. And he was coming back ten times as powerful.

Running had always made him feel like a coward, a failure. He'd have to forgive himself for that. There had been too much he didn't know—at the time. But he knew now. He knew now that he had been right then. He knew now that he had the support and ability to pick up where he left off. Finish the job. Find the vengeance he'd been denied so long.

The same vengeance he tried to find for others.

He let out a breath and signaled a passing flight attendant for a drink.

Dane rose from his seat, crossing in front of McConn and another passenger. He walked up the aisle to the lavatory and locked the door. He pressed one button on his cell phone and speed-dialed the president of the United States, Peter Cross.

An aid answered. "Yes?"

"It's Dane. Is he available?"

"One moment."

Cross came on the line. "Steve?"

"Good time?"

"I'm alone in the office, yes."

"Sir, I've just spoken with an old man who says he knows you."

"Calls himself Number One?"

"Exactly."

"Trust him, Steve."

"He told me some things about my father." Dane related the details of the conversation, leaving nothing out, including his current efforts.

Cross remained silent for a moment once Dane had finished.

"Are you there, sir?"

"Yes. I'll help all I can. Even now, whatever you need."

"It's better if I work on my own. I don't know who we can trust."

"Okay. But, Steve—"

"I'm aware of the consequences."

"You always are."

"Do you still light a candle for me, sir?"

"Every Sunday, without fail."

"Start lighting two. It's going to get bloody."

Nina met Dane and McConn at the airport wearing a thick and curly blonde wig.

"Actually looks good on you," Dane said.

"Our friends are looking for a brunette."

"Isn't everybody?"

They brought their carry-ons outside. Cars crowded the

curbside loading area. Buses spewed black exhaust into the sky. Nina stopped. "The Jag only has two seats."

McConn shook his head. "You two…guess I'm taking a cab."

Nina gave him the hotel address before she and Dane found the Jag in the crowded parking lot. She'd left the top up. Dane let her drive. He told her about The Trust and his father.

"I don't know what to say."

"Getting answers is priority one after we finish here, however it turns out."

They rode on without speaking. Dane watched the passing scenery without really seeing it.

He had to forgive himself for running away, but he couldn't.

"Tell me what you're thinking, Steve."

"Wondering why I ran," he said. "I was afraid of doing something that would send me to prison, but I've taken bigger risks since then. I was just scared."

"I don't think that's true."

"Why?"

"You couldn't have done then what you do now, because you hadn't done any of it yet. You were young and used to following the rules. Understand?"

"You mean running away, meeting you, all the stuff we've done, has been a training session?"

"I think you nailed it. And don't forget that *I* had a hand in getting you to this point," She smiled.

"What happens when it's done? What happens when I clear my father's name?"

"That's up to you. There are plenty of people like your father and plenty of others who turn them into victims. I don't have to tell you that. Plus, I think you like our lifestyle too much to give it up."

"True. I guess."

"You won't quit. *We* won't. Face it. This is the only way we feel *alive*."

She parked underneath the hotel overhang, and they had to wait only a few minutes for McConn to knock on the door to their room. While Dane answered, Nina stepped into the bathroom to remove the wig. She emerged with her natural dark hair cascading down her back.

Dane said, "So you approached Trent and his daughter, and this fellow Ivanov came calling?"

"It means Trent told Arkady. Gave him my card. The man is paranoid. He probably thinks, based on Arkady's influence, that the US government sent Blaze."

"And you were the next attempt," McConn said.

"Can we trust the daughter not to freak out?" Dane asked. "If we can get her to take us to her father, when Arkady isn't around, maybe we can make him understand what's happening."

"Our DHS IDs might help," McConn said. "With the daughter, anyway. Proof of official authority."

"If the Russians haven't frightened her, too," Dane said.

"I don't think so," said Nina. "Remember, she thought the interview was a good idea. I think she only knows what her father has told her. He hasn't told her what's really going on."

"He'd want to shield her from the unpleasant stuff, yeah," McConn agreed.

"We should intercept the daughter, like Nina wanted before Ivanov showed up," Dane said.

"I did manage to follow her home. Why don't we go over now?"

"Right. We're running out of time."

"I still can't fit in the Jag," McConn pointed out.

"And it might blow our cover is we use that car anyway," Dane said. "Everybody knows government agents don't roll around in F-Type convertibles."

Luckily the hotel had a small Enterprise office, where they were able to secure a proper sedan, a Chevy Impala, white in color, plain enough, in which McConn could sit as they drove to Colleen Trent's apartment.

Chapter Thirty-Eight

Traffic wasn't bad, and Dane found a guest parking spot near the young woman's building. A short elevator ride brought them to her door. Nina and McConn stood to the side as Dane knocked.

Colleen Trent answered. She wore pajamas with the Houston Texans' logo on the front and had her hair tied back. Her lack of makeup left light freckles on her cheeks exposed.

Dane introduced himself and let her see his DHS ID. It was coming in very handy. He might have to take back everything bad he'd ever said about federal employees.

"What is this about?" Colleen said.

"Your father and his deal with the Russians. He's in danger."

Concern flashed over her face as she opened the door. Dane introduced Nina and McConn, and Colleen's eyes widened in recognition of Nina.

"You're that reporter."

"She's with us," Dane said. "Can we sit down? Won't take long."

Colleen led them into the living room, where she turned off the TV and cleared space on the couch. Dane sat closest to her. She watched them eagerly.

Dane pulled no punches in describing the conspiracy. Colleen began to slouch as he spoke.

"We found out about Hess today," she said, "but they called it an accident."

"It's much worse than that. We were there. We failed to stop them *and* capture them."

Colleen straightened. "How do we stop them this time?"

"Only you can get us to your father. Without Arkady around."

"That's not possible tonight."

"Why?"

"Arkady is at the house with Dad. They're messing with Dad's train sets. Arkady loves those things. They'll be up all night."

"Tomorrow morning, then," Dane said.

"The demonstration is tomorrow morning."

Nina said, "That's when they'll strike."

"What do we do?" Colleen said.

"When will your father arrive at the office?" Dane said.

"Probably seven a.m. Arkady won't be there till noon. He *insisted* on noon."

"Then we see him at seven a.m.," Dane said.

"Meet me here," Colleen said. "I'll get you by the guards in front. Promise my father won't get hurt?"

"I promise," Dane said. "Only the ones who deserve it will get hurt."

Dane ignored the look Nina gave him. He knew what she was thinking, and she voiced the opinion as they drove away from the apartment complex. "I hope you can keep that promise, Steve," she said as she drove.

"We have to," Dane replied. "I'll do everything in my power to keep that promise."

Back at the hotel, Dane drew an approximate map of Trent's testing area while McConn brought up a satellite image of the Gulf of Mexico on his laptop.

"If that old man said Roxana Cavallos will be flying a helicopter," McConn said, "and Arkady insisted on noon, it means he needs the ship to be close enough for the chopper to reach without running out of gas. I figure two to three hours flight time. That puts the ship near the coast by three at the latest. Do you know what kind of ship? There may be more than one in the gulf."

"A cargo ship, most likely. They'll need a deck big enough to land a chopper and a hold big enough for the weapon," Dane said.

"It will have foreign markings," Nina said, "but not necessarily Russian. We used to use French vessels for this sort of thing."

"Why French?" McConn said.

"Easy paper trail and nobody argues with French ships. Everybody thinks the French are sissies."

"What about the crew?" Dane said. "Even if they speak French, they'll be armed."

"We can't let Arkady and the weapon get aboard," McConn said. "The three of us against a crew that size? We lose if that happens."

"No, we call the cavalry," Dane said.

"If those old men keep their word."

"They will," Dane said.

"Why are you so certain?"

"Gut feeling."

Alexander Arkady sat in the back corner of the bar at his hotel, the low light letting him blend with the shadows. He drank a cup of black coffee and stared at the big-screen television in a corner. The volume was off, but he read the subtitles of the program.

He'd had a nice evening with Trent and his trains, and he almost regretted the action that would take place the next day. Or in several hours. It was after 1 a.m.

Arkady went to the bar for a refill and returned to the table.

The cell phone in his jacket pocket vibrated. He answered.

"Yes?"

"It's Captain Sokolov."

"Yes, Captain. Are you still on schedule?"

"We are ahead of schedule. We are anchored outside US waters."

"How long will it take to reach the rendezvous point?"

"Two hours. We can move up the timetable if you'd like."

Arkady tapped his lip and considered the idea. Cavallos and Roxana were ready. Trent's weapon would be ready early. It would not be hard to accelerate things and cut down their exposure on the climax of the mission.

"Let's do that," Arkady said. "Be at the rendezvous at ten a.m."

"We'll be there. Good luck, comrade."

Arkady hung up and smiled.

The M-113, with the 680c mounted on top, rolled across the open field of Trent's testing ground, approaching a target about 100 yards away. Another World War Two–era tank, fully intact, sat down range, awaiting pulverization.

The M-113 rocked side to side as it rolled over some

rough patches in the dirt, the slow trailing pickup full of engineers hitting the same bumps.

Blue sky above, clear. Bright sun. One of the engineers remarked that the sun and crisp morning air made it the perfect day for a demonstration.

Theodore Trent paced the floor of his office, nervous sweat dotting his forehead.

The potential for a signed deal with the Russians certainly excited him, but he tempered the thrill with his knowledge that the US had twice tried to interfere and probably would again, either before or after the deal.

He had to maintain an air of confidence. This was the critical moment. Everything he had worked for. His company was at stake. His legacy. His daughter's future.

Especially his daughter's future. Deep down he felt like he had held her back from getting on with whatever other kind of life she wanted. He hadn't insisted she stay after the passing of her mother, but he hadn't told her to leave, either. Had he taken advantage of her sense of obligation to him? If he had, it wasn't overtly. Once Trent Defense was flush again, they'd have a heart to heart talk about her moving on. It was only right.

He wiped his forehead with a handkerchief and—

The office door swung open. Trent turned in surprise. Arkady and Ivanov entered, both as stoic as ever. The big Cossack shut the door.

"Alexander."

"We decided to show up early," Arkady said. "The hotel was boring. I hope that isn't a problem."

"Of course not." Trent actually welcomed the distraction. If he was focused on making Arkady happy, he wouldn't think of the other problems.

"My car's out front. We can go out and watch them set up at the test site."

Trent picked up the desk phone.

It was 7:05 a.m.

Chapter Thirty-Nine

Colleen did her best, but the traffic defeated her. She didn't pull into the parking lot of Trent HQ until 7:15.

She slowed for the gate guard to see her, saying to him, "Is my father here?"

"Yes, those two Russians are here, too."

"Thanks, Chris."

Colleen drove through the open gate.

"Why are they early?" Dane said from the back.

"Don't know."

Colleen led Dane, Nina and McConn through the front lobby and down a hall to Trent's office, where his secretary said he wasn't alone. Colleen didn't tell her that she already knew.

Dane told McConn to wait with the receptionist. Just in case. The young woman behind the desk wasn't stupid. She read the hard expressions of Dane, McConn, and Nina, and started visibly becoming nervous. Something wrong? Colleen told her all was well but to be ready to call security. McConn offered her a smile, but she only sat down quickly and couldn't find anything to do with her shaking hands.

Colleen reached for her father's door and went in, Dane and Nina following.

Trent and the Russians snapped their attention, med conversation, to Colleen and her companions.

Colleen announced, "Dad, you can't sell to these people."

"What is the meaning of this?" Arkady said.

"Arkady is here to steal the 680c and frame us for blowing up Hess Laboratories."

"That is *insane*," Trent said. "Colleen, what are you thinking?"

Arkady and Ivanov fell silent, but there was a trace of a smile on Ivanov's face as he looked at Nina.

"This man," Colleen said, gesturing to Dane, "is from Homeland Security. He knows their whole plan."

Arkady laughed. "That man is an imposter, and so is his companion. They are wanted criminals. Con artists."

"Careful, Alexander," Nina said. "Why would you know that?"

"Mr. Trent," Dane said, "your daughter is telling the truth."

"I don't know who you are, but I want you out of my office. You too, Colleen."

"But, Dad—"

"Not another word."

Arkady said, "If I may have your attention."

The Hawk leveled a pistol at Colleen Trent. She made a sound and stepped behind Dane.

"Alexander—"

"Quiet, Theo. In the heat of the moment, I did slip. Your daughter is indeed correct."

The color drained from Trent's face and he dropped into his desk chair. "I don't understand. Does this mean—"

"I played you like a fiddle, yes. Now don't get too comfortable." Arkady gave Ivanov instructions in Russian. The big man went to Dane and relieved him of the Detonics Scoremaster. Nina handed over her Smith & Wesson. Ivanov held a gun in each hand and retook his spot beside Arkady.

Arkady holstered his gun. "I have a date with the test site. Ivanov will keep you all company for the next few minutes."

"What happens then?" Dane said.

"You'll see," Arkady said. "Your arrival is quite lucky for me. We will much easier be able to sell the story we want with you two here."

Arkady left and shut the door quietly behind him.

Ivanov backed up until he touched the wall.

Nina said, "Guess the knives didn't work out?"

"Shut up."

"Tell me something, big guy," Dane said. "What's Nina's nickname?"

"Stephen!"

"Hey, if we're gonna be shot, I want to go knowing what they called you."

"It's not important," she said.

"Of course it is."

"You do not need to *know*."

"Why are you keeping secrets from me?"

"Enough!" Ivanov said. "We called her Nina the Bitch."

Nina let out a sigh. "Here we go."

"That's all?" Dane said. "Really, that's all? We had that big build-up for one of the biggest let-downs ever? Hey, you big dumb ox, *I* could have told you that."

Nina cursed in Russian. Ivanov laughed.

"This isn't funny!" Colleen said. She crossed to her father. He stood and she put her arms around him. Trent pulled her close and his eyes pleaded with Dane.

"Relax," Dane told them.

A knock on the door. "Pizza!"

"Somebody order a pie?" Dane said.

Another knock. "It's getting cold! Ain't got all day."

Ivanov told Nina to move over to the desk. He told Dane to answer the door and stayed a little bit behind him, the Detonics .45 aimed at Dane's back.

Dane opened the door and wedged his body into the opening.

"Yes?"

"Pizza delivery," McConn said.

"We're all lactose intolerant, wrong office."

"The cheese is gluten-free."

McConn handed Dane a gun. Dane turned and shot Ivanov in the left eye. The big Cossack feel like a chopped tree and landed hard on the floor.

"Took long enough," Nina said.

Dane gave back McConn's gun and helped himself to his .45 and returned the S&W to Nina. The receptionist entered, her wide eyes and open mouth matching Colleen's. Trent breathed evenly as he took in the scene.

"Todd," Dane said, "how did Arkady not see you when he left?"

"The receptionist let me hide under her desk."

Nina laughed.

"Call the police," Dane told Colleen. To Trent, "Do you have a car?"

Trent stuttered at first but said, "Out front."

"You two stay and coordinate with the cops. If anybody asks—"

"You're on my security team."

"Send them, too," Dane said. "We'll need the help."

Arkady stopped his car a few feet from the M-113.

As he climbed out, he heard a helicopter approaching from the south.

Two engineers at the 680c stopped performing their adjustments and watched Arkady.

"Where is Mr. Trent?" one said.

"Indisposed." Arkady raised his gun and shot each man in the forehead.

He quick-stepped to the bunker as the other two engineers ran. Arkady shot the first man, the other tripping over the body to sprawl at the Hawk's feet. The engineer started to rise; two rounds from Arkady's pistol flattened him again. This time he didn't try to get up.

Arkady looked back at the rising dust cloud behind an approaching vehicle.

He grunted and spoke into a walkie-talkie taken from a pocket. The chopper was getting closer.

"We have unauthorized visitors," Arkady said into the handheld unit.

"We see them," said Roxana.

The chopper dipped to the right. The side door opened and Arkady saw Cavallos lean out with a machine gun.

Chapter Forty

"Chopper!" Nina shouted.

The Boeing CH-47 Chinook had twin rotors and the capability to lift 50,000 pounds. A formidable machine. The aircraft swung perpendicular to the Lincoln. Dane slammed the brakes. The first burst from the machine gun strafed the dirt in front of the incoming Lincoln MZK as it skidded to a stop. The chopper swung around in a circle. Dane floored the pedal and Trent's car lurched forward, throwing all three back against their seats. Cavallos's second burst spayed across the ground.

"We're gonna run out of luck eventually," McConn said.

Dane aimed the MKZ at Arkady. Less than 50 yards. Machine gun fire hammered next to the car, finally cutting across the hood. The Lincoln lurched again, this time forward with Dane, Nina and McConn straining against the seat belts, before stopping. The chopper flew on and turned back toward Arkady and the M-113. Dust and smoke swirled everywhere.

Cavallos and Roxana had secured the CH-47 with a magnetic towline that lowered from the bottom. The magnet would hold the steel M-113 as long as it took to make the rendezvous with Captain Sokolov's ship.

Cavallos watched the smoking car. More vehicles were converging on the test site from the main building, no doubt Trent's security forces reacting to the arrival of the chopper. It certainly didn't belong there.

Roxana worked the controls and maneuvered the helicopter over the M-113. She pulled a lever that lowered the towline at the same time as Cavallos released a rope ladder, which hit the ground first. The magnet stuck to the M-113 with a loud clang that Cavallos heard over the noise of the whipping twin rotors.

Arkady grabbed on to the ladder and began the long climb. The chopper dipped as the M-113 left the ground, but Roxana straightened out, compensating for the weight with more power. Both the M-113 and Arkady ascended toward the chopper.

Cavallos watched the three people from the damaged car approach. He fired two bursts, the trio splitting up and rolling for cover. They made no attempt to return fire with their handguns. The chopper was too far away for their return fire to cause any damage.

The motor running the tow cable let out a low moan once they secured the M-113 to the undercarriage, and shortly after, a gasping Arkady climbed into view. Cavallos helped him aboard and slid the side door closed.

Arkady crawled onto a seat, panting.

"Harder than it looks," the Hawk said.

"Ivanov?"

"If Dane and the woman got away, it means he's dead. Let's go."

Roxana already had the CH-47 on course for the Gulf of Mexico. ETA two hours. She didn't care one bit about the survival of the Russian Cossack, really. What she cared about was that somebody was after them. Somebody who threatened the safe harbor she and her husband had been promised by the panting Russian who had yet to catch his breath. She steered the chopper with a grim set to her face. They had to deal with yet another problem, but maybe after, they could find sanctuary.

Dane, still flat on the ground, dirt clinging to the sweat on his face, watched the helicopter vanish into a small speck in the blue sky. Nina and McConn, equally dirty, rejoined him as the other vehicles bringing Trent's security force arrived and skidded to a stop. More dust drifted around them. As the men piled out, Dane went up to the team leader.

"Does Trent have a chopper?"

"Yes."

"Where is it?"

"At the airport halfway across town."

"We need to get there *now*."

Trent drove them in a company car. He drove hard and fast and blew through two red lights to get to the freeway, and then he drove the next ten miles at twenty over the limit.

He'd called the hangar ahead of time to have the on-site mechanic prep the helicopter for flight.

The hangar used by Trent's company sat at the western edge of the airport. Trent used a key card to get through the security gate and brought them to the hangar. The Bell chopper sat outside, the mechanic checking the oil. Dane, Nina and McConn followed Trent to the helicopter.

Trent explained that Dane and the other two wanted

to give the chopper a quick check ride, as it might be up for sale. The mechanic didn't seem to care, but he also asked no further questions. He did announce that the Bell was ready. McConn, who would fly, made some cursory checks of his own.

Nina and McConn climbed aboard. Trent grabbed Dane's arm.

"How are you going to stop them?"

"I don't know."

"Are you coming back? The authorities—"

"If you have trouble, I know some guys who can pull strings."

McConn started the motor, and the rotors began a whining rotation as the engine fired.

"Good luck," Dane said.

"To you as well," said Trent.

Dane hopped in the back and pulled the door shut.

They wore headsets to communicate over the intercom.

Nina studied a map on her iPhone. "Head southeast," she said. "That will take us out to the gulf."

"I can't go above fifteen hundred feet because of other traffic," McConn said, "so we should get out there in two hours or so."

"They have a thirty-minute head start," Dane said.

"Is that enough time to land and unload?"

"Probably," Dane said. He sat back and looked out the window. The passing scenery held no interest, and Corpus Christi looked like any other US city. He watched it anyway.

Presently he caught himself tapping his right foot. He stopped. The thrill of the chase, the possibility of defeat, turning that defeat into victory, filled him with excitement.

Nina was right. He was *alive.* Once old scores were settled, Dane would only have more of a reason to carry on as is. He could never go back to any official duty, same as he couldn't stop breathing.

He said into the intercom, "You were right, honey."

"I usually am."

"You really do earn that nickname, you know."

She laughed.

"Am I missing something?" McConn said.

"Just fly, Todd," Dane said.

Chapter Forty-One

The cargo chopper had gone "feet wet" two hours and ten minutes after leaving Trent's campus, and Cavallos scanned the ocean water below. The gulf was full of cargo ships, yachts and sailboats. Cavallos ignored the other craft and focused his binoculars on the cargo ships. He wanted one with a clear deck.

Cavallos settled on a ship with an empty deck and French identification and pointed it out to Arkady. The Hawk took the binoculars for his own examination.

"That's it," he said.

Cavallos told Roxana and she turned left, one pass over the ship's superstructure, announcing her arrival. She continued circling. A flag man on the roof of the superstructure signaled by waving flags that they would have the hold open shortly.

It took some time, but a section of the deck near the bow eventually opened, the hinged cargo doors rising upward like a trapdoor in reverse. Roxana watched a second flag man, who stood on the deck, signal with the flags. She had to fight the drift of the chopper and the movement of the ship. Despite its size, the waves still rocked the vessel, with the bow rising and falling.

The flag man finally crossed his arms. Roxana threw the lever that activated the tow cable and slowly lowered the M-113 into the hold. There was plenty of clearance in the opening, so the movement of the ship posed no danger. The M-113 was not going to crash into the side.

But the vehicle did have a specific place in the hold, and Roxana corrected per the flag man's instructions. When he waved the all clear by whipping both flags to and fro in rapid succession, she disengaged the magnet and retracted the tow cable.

She circled the ship again as the deck doors swung closed. Then the flag man waved another set of signals: cleared to land. Roxana set the chopper down on the deck and shut off the motor as deckhands secured the helicopter to the deck with ropes and chains.

Arkady stepped out a happy man. Despite the complications of John Blaze and Steve Dane and Nina Talikova, the plan was more than successful, and the Motherland now had a DEW to reverse-engineer and duplicate.

Cavallos and his wife had their own reason to be happy as well.

Captain Sokolov—sixtyish, a short man with dark hair and a face weathered by decades of sun and salt water— welcomed them aboard and then led the trio below decks. He said they'd begin steaming for home immediately.

Cavallos liked the sound of the word "home."

The captain showed them to their quarters first, then to the cantina. Arkady wanted coffee right away, while Cavallos and Roxana needed to change and shower.

Cavallos stretched out on the narrow bed while Roxana splashed in the tiny shower. Their room was small and the ceiling low, but they were on the way to something better. Sanctuary.

"Hey," Roxana called from the shower. "We have limited hot water."

"So?"

"By the time I'm done, you won't have any."

Cavallos sighed. "Wouldn't that be a shame." He stood up and went in to join her.

"We're gonna have a gas problem, Steve," McConn said.

"How long before we absolutely positively have to turn back?"

"Thirty-two minutes and forty-nine seconds."

"I appreciate the precision."

Dane wasn't surprised. They had only just cleared the coast. They were over US waters, with Dane and Nina scanning the ocean. McConn had to stay low, since they had no binoculars.

Dane noted that the cargo ships were all loaded, decks stacked with rectangular containers.

"Our ship won't have containers on deck," he said. "Look for bare decks."

"With a chopper," Nina added. "If they've landed by now, that will be the only thing on the deck."

The water rushed below, McConn holding steady at the controls. He maneuvered throughout the gulf traffic, but none of the cargo ships matched what they sought.

"Could they have made Cuba?" McConn said.

"Who knows?" Nina said. "Maybe they weren't as close to the coast as we thought."

"We can talk in circles and it's not going to help us," Dane said. The three of them fell silent again. McConn headed for the open ocean.

Dane's phone chirped. He looked at the text message. A set of coordinates and the words "Number One" at the end. Dane showed the text to McConn.

"Can you use these?"

McConn took the phone. "Yup."

McConn set the coordinates on the dash GPS and guided the helicopter in a long left turn. When he finally leveled out, he passed back the phone. "Clock ticking on gas."

"We'll get there in time."

Dane took out the Detonics Scoremaster and checked it, moving two spare magazines from his shoulder harness to the right pocket of his jacket.

"Tally ho!" McConn shouted.

Dane and Nina looked ahead. The dark dot of the enemy ship lay ahead.

"What's the plan?"

"Land on the deck," Dane said.

"We only have pistols," Nina said.

Dane mashed his teeth together. There was no good way to handle this.

"We have to try," Dane said.

"Let's not get killed before we finish that other business," Nina said.

"We can't let them go."

Nina gave him a look that Dane ignored.

He could at least get a picture and send it to President Cross. Let the Navy take over.

McConn held the chopper on course. The ship grew larger as they neared. McConn dropped low and zoomed over the deck. He turned back. Dane popped open his door. The force of the air outside tried to press it closed, but he twisted in the seat to push it open enough to aim the .45.

He fired at the deck hands rushing up from below. They carried automatic weapons and shot at the chopper.

"Around again," Dane said. "I want to get a picture and we'll go back."

"We have two minutes," McConn said.

McConn aimed the helicopter at the back of the super-structure. He closed the distance quickly. As the chopper flew the length of the deck, Dane set his pistol aside, stuck out his phone and took pictures, focusing on the hull ID and name of the ship.

A burst of automatic weapon fire from the deck punched through the chopper's floor. Nina screamed. Dane saw blood spatter on her face. But it wasn't her blood. The bullet had hit McConn. One of the slugs coming through the floor had split open his right leg.

Chapter Forty-Two

Dane shifted and leaned between the two front seats to see the damage when the chopper lurched left, McConn's hand slipping from the controls as he raced to right the helicopter.

The lurch flung the unsecured Dane backward into the door. The still-unlatched door opened as his weight struck it, and he fell through the air toward the cold ocean below.

Dane rolled over in mid-air, taking a diving form. The impact would hurt. There was nothing he could do about that. He had to *literally* play the hand he had been dealt, and that meant taking a swim.

He slammed into the water hard, the cold shock pummeling his system, but he followed through on the dive and arced upward, breaking the surface a few yards from the ship's hull. Deck hands were already on the edge of the top rail pointing at him.

A wave washed over Dane's head and he went under for a moment before springing back up to the surface. He treaded water wondering what to do now. And then the deck hands started lowering a lifeboat into the water, two men with weapons aboard. The outboard motor rumbled and the boat steered Dane's way.

Dane glanced at the chopper he'd fallen from. McConn and Nina were already heading back to land. They had no choice. Neither did Dane. He'd face the enemy alone, no back-up, no guarantee of victory.

Dane laughed as the boat chugged closer.

"Can you still fly?" Nina said.

McConn grimaced, blood spurting from the hole in his leg. More of the blood had spilled onto the floor, and the seat itself, McConn sliding forward and pushing himself back.

"Gonna be messy but I think so!"

"We can't just leave him!"

"We'll all be dead if I don't get us on the ground!"

Nina took off her jacket and used a pocketknife to slice a strip of fabric. She fashioned a tourniquet for McConn's leg and tightened it. McConn turned the helicopter back toward land.

Nina said, "We have to do something when we land."

"He'll be fine."

Nina looked back and saw Dane's phone and gun on the floor. She picked up the phone and found the text message from Number One.

"Let's see if these three old guys are as good as Steve thinks they are," she said.

Dane bobbed up and down with the waves as the lifeboat finally reached him. One of the two on board pointed an automatic rifle at his face. He gestured for Dane to climb aboard, and Dane rolled over the side to fall flat on the floor. The man at the rudder steered the boat back to the ship, where they connected with the lift cables and the

crew up top raised the lifeboat.

Dane lay still, gasping, choking on salt water. He rolled over and retched several times. The goons in the boat didn't bother him. The boat bumped against the hull as it rose. The rush of wind as the boat rose higher felt good against Dane's wet face. His clothes clung to his body and made it hard to move.

On deck, more guards lifted Dane out of the boat. He didn't help and let them carry his full weight, his feet dragging on the rough deck. He wasn't going to make it easy for them.

They carried him across the deck to the superstructure at the rear. It loomed larger as they approached. Already Dane had developed a few strategies in mind for sinking the ship. Having Trent's laser weapon on board might be the ace he needed.

The door slammed and locked. Dane lay on itchy carpet. The crew apparently used the room for storage, as an abundance of broken chairs and other pieces of discarded furniture sat stacked halfway to the ceiling.

He lay face down breathing the odd smell of the carpet, his wet clothes dripping, leaving a wet outline of his body. He wouldn't be moving very fast with those wet clothes. His plan required fast movement.

Dane rolled over, his clothes sloshing, and stared at the ceiling for a while.

He didn't bother trying to find a chair to sit on, and his examining much of the junk revealed nothing he could use as a weapon. He found a clear spot on the wall and collapsed. He stared at the door. Eventually he had looked so long that the door opened.

Arkady entered and regarded Dane with a flat expression.

"I must be a cat," Dane said.

Arkady shook his head. "The Dane wit. Tell me why."

"Every cat knows that if you stare at a door long enough, somebody will open it."

"I'm sure somebody is amused by that, Mr. Dane. Not I."

"What brings you here, Arkady? Sorry I don't have any refreshments. The place is also a bit of a mess. I wasn't expecting company."

Arkady took two more steps forward. He left the door open. An armed guard stood outside near the doorway. Dane made eye contact with the man and smiled. The guard was young. Dane held his eyes. The guard blinked.

Arkady put his hands in the pockets of his black slacks.

"I wish I had your lady friend as well."

"She'll be along with the cavalry."

"Nobody is coming to rescue you, Mr. Dane."

"Who says the cavalry will be official?"

"I forgot, you're a pirate of sorts. There's no way a force could be quickly organized to take this ship, and if you had that to begin with, you would not have flown over in a helicopter armed only with handguns. You are on your own this time."

"Just me and my wit. You're all doomed."

"I'm thinking my superior in Moscow would like to know what's in your head," Arkady said. "You may have something of value locked in there."

"You're not going to torture me? Is that what you're saying? I'll be disappointed if I'm not smacked in the balls with a carpet beater. It's standard practice in these situations."

"Maybe later."

"Talk about not being prepared, Arkady."

"Don't bother thinking of escape. Every deck hand is armed. You are outnumbered and outgunned. You'll also catch pneumonia in those clothes."

"If you want me alive, some new threads would be nice."

"You'll have to take your chances."

"Fine, then."

"Besides, if you *are* like a cat, you still have a few lives to spare."

Arkady's chuckle sounded like a snort as he left the room, closing the door. The lock slammed into place.

A locked door, one guard, no available weapons and wet clothes. As Dane ran down the list, he found little to be hopeful about. Ideas would come. He already knew what to do once he escaped, but he had to get out first.

Was Nina organizing something? A call to The Trust might pay dividends, and show whether or not they were really worthwhile, despite President Cross's assurances. Dane figured they were his only shot. What he did before they showed up would only make it easier when they did arrive.

First, he needed to get out of his "cell" and take the guard's weapon.

Chapter Forty-Three

McConn struggled to keep the chopper aloft, dipping and swaying as he flew toward land. Nina grabbed the co-pilot controls. The chopper pitched left. McConn shouted, "Whoa, careful!" He adjusted the controls and leveled out. Nina softened her grip. As soon as they cleared land, McConn steered for an open space in which to set down. They drifted over the JFK Memorial Causeway and circled over more water to the open fields on Padre Island. McConn set the skids on the ground just beyond Park Road 22, in a dirt lot in a Packery Channel Park near a cluster of buildings.

Nina leaped out and ran around to McConn's side. He slumped in the chair, legs splayed and arms limp, his head back on the headrest.

"Great landing," she said, unstrapping the safety belts holding him to the seat. He groaned as she helped him exit. Nina placed McConn on the ground, flat on his back, and bundled up her jacket for a pillow.

He started shaking. Going into shock. Nina rummaged through the clutter in the back cargo area and found a blanket. She threw it over him.

Nina grabbed her cell and called for help. She could explain things to the local law enforcement once paramedics had secured McConn. She told the police operator that her helicopter had crashed, leaving the pilot injured.

Then she dialed Number One on Dane's phone.

"Mr. Dane?" the old man said.

"No, the better half."

"Ah, Miss Talikova. What's wrong?"

She told him Dane was alone on the Russian ship with Arkady, who was getting away with the laser weapon. She had help on the way for her situation, but Steve needed help for his.

"I'll alert the Coast Guard, Miss Talikova. Help is on the way."

"You just snap your fingers, huh?"

"A lot of people owe me favors. I'll be in touch."

The call ended and Nina checked on McConn. Still conscious, breathing hard but steadily.

"How bad is it?" she said.

"I'm lying on a rock. Hurts worse than my leg."

Sirens in the distance.

"Hang in there, help is coming."

A Coast Guard HC-144A Ocean Sentry, out of Clearwater, Florida, turned from its southerly direction and headed into the gulf at full throttle.

The pilot, Commander Greg Macedo, a twenty-year veteran of the Guard, had received the radio call directly from his superior back at HQ. Drop everything and head for these coordinates. Look for a cargo ship. Observe and report. A pair of choppers with two squads from the Atlantic Strike Team was also on the way.

Macedo and his co-pilot, Chief Warrant Officer Mitch

Storey, didn't argue. "Probably drug dealers," Macedo said. Storey's calculations on the GPS showed that at average speed, the target would hit Cuban waters in just under three hours.

Commander Macedo figured it was a big target if two squads of Guard commandos were required. CWO Storey said they'd have the perfect seat for the show.

Time to target: thirty minutes.

Dane started feeling better after a while but also began to shiver because of the wet clothes. He sat up and tore off his shirt, buttons flying, the wet fabric ripping easily. His bare upper body, still wet, felt much colder exposed. But now he had formed his action plan, and the time had come to put it to work.

He couldn't go to Russia, of course, and not only because he hated the taste of borscht.

Dane stood up and moved his legs about, testing his freedom of movement. While he could run, the tight slacks clung to his skin, limiting his speed. He had an idea for fixing that but first needed a knife.

He regarded the door a moment. The usual tricks to get the guard's attention wouldn't work. A slight change to an old routine might prove useful, however. Dane pounded on the door.

"Hey!"

"What?" the guard said from the other side.

"I need a bucket. I don't think Arkady wants to clean piss out of the carpet."

No reply.

Dane banged a fist on the door. "Hey!"

Silence.

Dane stepped back with hands on hips. Maybe he was

plain out of luck. Was borscht really that bad?

The guard knocked. "Get back."

"Okay."

The door opened and the trooper placed a small bucket on the floor. Dane snatched it up.

"This won't work."

"You wanted a bucket."

"It won't work."

"Why?"

"Because your head won't fit."

The guard clawed for his sidearm as Dane brought the bucket up and down onto his head. The rim of the bucket jammed on the guard's skull like a fez. He cried out and Dane slammed a fist into his solar plexus. The guard doubled over as Dane brought his knee up into his face. Teeth crunched. Dane let the man fall, yanked off the bucket and hit him with it again. The guard lay flat, unconscious.

Dane shut the door, then knelt to examine the guard's gear. Combat harness with radio. Handgun: a SIG-Sauer P-226. Submachine gun: SR-2 Veresk, a Russian make. Spare ammo. Dane also found a very sharp pocketknife and started cutting the slacks above the knee. By the time he discarded the scraps, he'd turned the pants into crude shorts with jagged cuffs. High fashion. He looked like the Incredible Hulk if the green rage thing hadn't worked out, but his clothes still tore. He next stripped the trooper of his gear. He found the radio and held it in his hand as though it were solid gold.

He had to sink the ship. The best way to do that was to find Trent's weapon and use it to blast a hole through the bottom. If he was a laser weapon, where would he hide? Roxana Cavallos had landed the CH-47 near the bow. The weapon had to be underneath. The superstructure, where he'd been taken, was at the stern. Dane had to make his way along the entire length of the ship.

He took a deep breath and stepped through the doorway, a commando in short pants. Maybe the ungodly would laugh themselves to death and save him the work of shooting them.

Stranger things had happened.

Chapter Forty-Four

Dane entered a small room bare of furniture but filled with empty boxes and obviously broken and inoperative equipment, old computers and panels—junk. At the next door he peeked out to see an empty hallway. Fluorescent lighting in the ceiling, yellow walls, thin carpeting. It looked like any office hallway. Other doors lined the hall. Dane left the junk room, his wet socks squishing in his equally wet shoes. He heard no voices or activity; no light crept from under any of the other doors. At the end of the hall he saw a port window and squished over to look out. Still some daylight left. He appeared to be on the middle level of the superstructure. Going back the way he had come, he found a stairwell behind one of the doors.

Dane paused to listen. No obvious sounds but the low throb of the engines far below. Nothing on the radio.

He could venture up and try to take the bridge, then wait for the cavalry. Very tempting. If the other troops around the ship made a counter-attack, he'd have very few options. On a battleship he could simply lock the doors, but he had no idea if the cargo ship was similarly equipped. Hell, the hallways had carpeting. Navy ships did not. At least not the ones he'd visited.

Dane started down the stairwell. Some chatter came over the radio. Hourly security check. The head of the security team called out to each squad, who answered, and when the boss started repeating a name, Dane knew his time was now very limited. The boss was calling the trooper Dane had conked. The head of security communicated with another team, and Dane heard enough of the conversation to know the team was on its way to investigate.

Assuming the team was close, the stairwell might well become a death trap. Dane found the safety on the Veresk and switched it to Fire.

He advanced down the steps, pausing at each landing. When he reached the third landing down from where he had started, a hatch below squeaked open. Two troopers, talking. Dane squatted in the corner. The troopers started up, their boots scraping on the steps. Dane tucked the Veresk's stock into his shoulder. The boots grew louder.

The troopers' heads appeared first as they reached the landing below and turned to come Dane's way. Dane fired, the Veresk loud in the confined space, the muzzle flash blinding. He let off the trigger. The two troopers lay dead on the landing.

Dane hustled forward, stepping over the bodies, and down the next flight of stairs. He passed the open hatch. A stencil on the hatch read "Level D." How many levels till he reached the area below decks?

The radio sparked to life. Somebody reporting the shooting. Names were called and repeated, over and over. Then the alarm sounded, a loud Klaxon, and Dane moved faster. At Level F he opened the hatch to figure out his location. Another hallway. He started down again and stopped.

A hatch below clanged open and boots rushed up the stairs. Dane ran back to Level F and entered the hallway, closing the hatch. No lock.

He dashed down the hall to a door, turned the knob and entered.

The head of security continued to blather over the radio.

Marco Cavallos listened in his cabin with growing irritation.

"What do you think?" Roxana said.

"Dane got out. If he isn't going for the bridge, he'll head for the weapon."

"He won't make it to the hold. Too far to go."

"It's *Steve Dane* we're talking about."

"He's alone."

"That just makes him even more dangerous."

Cavallos picked up a phone from the wall and dialed Arkady's cabin.

"Yes?" the Hawk said.

"Are you listening to the mess on the radio?"

"Yes."

"Dane has more than likely escaped."

"Agreed."

"Tell the captain to put me in charge."

"What can you do that his men can't?"

"Think like Dane."

The radio crackled again, urgent chatter from troops on the top deck. Captain Sokolov responded with an acknowledgment.

"Is it the Navy?" Cavallos said.

"Coast Guard," Arkady said. "You can bet the Navy will follow. I'll tell the captain to put you in charge of chasing Dane."

Dane entered the room off the hall and startled the two sailors inside who were sitting at tables against the wall. One jumped up and rushed Dane while the other reached for a phone. Dane clubbed the charging sailor with the Veresk SMG, stepping aside as the man collided with the wall. Dane closed the gap to the second man as he hurriedly dialed. A second swing of the SMG knocked the sailor out cold. He collapsed onto his desk and then fell to the floor.

Dane glanced at their paperwork and glowing computer monitors but saw nothing of value in the Cyrillic notes. The emergency map of the ship that hung on the wall grabbed his attention, and he eagerly studied it. Chatter over the radio. Dane lowered the volume and listened. Somebody up top had spotted a Coast Guard plane. Redirected by The Trust?

Dane examined the map some more, looking for the engine control room. Now that the Coast Guard had found them, Dane didn't want the ship to slip away before the heavy hitters arrived.

Another conversation over the two-way. Cavallos was taking over the search for the prisoner. The captain ordered all troops to Level B.

Of course, they knew he was listening.

He wasn't going to just walk into an ambush, but he might as well make sure they were short a few guys.

Dane looked at the map once more, left the room, and went down the hall to the stairwell door. Two troopers were on their way. Dane leaned against the doorway and fired a burst. The shots echoed loudly and whined off the steel walls to bounce back and forth, one bullet cutting through one of the troopers. The other ascended faster. Dane fired another trio of rounds that brought down the trooper.

Dane ran down two levels of stairs and pulled open the hatch to the engine room. Weapon to his shoulder, he moved forward and scanned left to right. The noise level in the crowded space was deafening, the growl of the engines filling the room. Pipes climbed up the walls and across the ceiling, pumps and electronics units covering the rest of the space. Dane checked the wall alcoves, the empty adjoining workshop. Not even a skeleton crew?

Dane squeezed between pieces of equipment to a railing. Over the side and one level down, he saw the engine. It took up most of the floor, a long cylindrical cocoon with pipes arcing over the top. The loud throb shook the floor and the rail. Dane crossed to the control room, more electronics consoles along the wall. He looked for a big red off switch, but of course it wasn't that easy. A turret-style desk at one end seemed the most promising spot, and he did find an emergency cutoff button shielded by a plastic cover. He flipped the cover and pressed the button. Another alarm sounded, two short blasts, then the beast one level below shuddered. The room shook. Then the motor closed down with a sigh. The panels lit up with flashing lights, computer monitors displaying various prompts and awaiting action, but the ship had now effectively stopped. It might be only a brief delay, but he would take that.

Dane slipped out of the control room and stopped short. He wasn't alone any longer. Four troops rushed into the engine room. Dane dove for cover as their assault weapons spit flame.

Chapter Forty-Five

The shots bounced around the engine room, one striking a wall pipe.
The pipe cracked and steam hissed from the opening.

Dane crawled on his stomach, catching glimpses of the troopers' legs as he peeked around the cluster of now quiet pumps he hid behind. The troops made no sound.

The steam continued hissing, a layer of it gathering below the ceiling.

Dane rose and fired at one of the troopers, stitching his chest. Dane dropped and moved forward to another hiding spot. Return fire echoed, ricochets bouncing in deadly random directions. A stray shot struck a wall panel, which exploded and sent a puff of black smoke into the steam cloud.

The steam cloud started to spread. Dane fired two blind bursts to let the ricochets drive the troopers to cover. He ran for the rail overlooking the engine, found a ladder and climbed down, breathing hard as he hustled quickly down the rungs. On the lower level he reloaded the SMG and ran for the hatch on the opposite side. He looked back to see the three remaining troops rushing the rail. He hit the floor and rolled under the engine as they opened fire. He aimed out from underneath and fired back, the motor's heat only inches from his skin. One trooper fell. The others ran for the ladder. Dane rolled out, jumped up and shot the trooper coming down. As the body hit the floor, the other, still at the rail, fired. One of his shots struck Dane's weapon, splitting open the action and blazing a furrow across the back of Dane's right hand. Dane dropped the weapon and ran at a crouch along the length of the engine, taking out the SIG pistol and firing twice at the last trooper, who fell backward off the ladder and struck the floor with a loud thud.

Dane ran to the troopers and collected both Veresk submachine guns and their ammo. He jammed the SIG-Sauer in his belt. With one Veresk slung across his back and the other in hand, he ran back to the hatch and slipped through, finding another narrow passage, a new set of steps ahead. Dane's shoes squished less as he ran down the steps, and the radio remained silent.

Arkady joined Captain Sokolov on the bridge. The captain ran the bridge with three other sailors, including their chief engineer. The three sailors sat at their assigned positions while Sokolov peered through binoculars at the sky.

Arkady ran to the bridge when he heard the engines halt. The ship, stopped, rocked with the waves.

"The plane is only circling," Sokolov reported.

The chief engineer tried to get the troops in the engine room on the radio, no reply.

Cavallos radioed that they had the DEW surrounded and secured.

Arkady folded his arms. "Is there a way to shoot down that plane?"

Sokolov gave him a shocked expression. "That would

be an act of war."

"I've already committed one act of war already today."

The chief engineer said, "I'm working through the over-rides to restart the engines. As far as I can tell, the engine hasn't been damaged."

None of that was good enough for Arkady, and he said so before turning to find an empty chair at one of the consoles. He sat down slowly.

The chief engineer clapped his hands. "Engine running!"

The floor rumbled as the motor reached full power. The captain ordered the helmsman to resume course. The sailor punched buttons on his console and eased the throttle lever forward.

Arkady didn't leave his chair, and said, "Can we make international waters before American ships arrive?"

"At full throttle, I think so."

"I don't want you to *think*."

"The engines will take it," the chief engineer said. He read more information on his monitors. "No damage. He just turned it off."

"We'll get there then," Sokolov said.

The helmsman said, "Will the Americans sink us, sir?"

Arkady answered. "They won't, but Dane might."

"Would he take that chance?" Sokolov said.

"He'll die with us," Arkady said. "He stopped the ship to buy time, but now he'll need another plan. It's imperative that Cavallos stop him before he reaches the laser. That's the only way he can sink this ship." Arkady took out his two-way. "Cavallos."

"Here, sir."

"Dane's coming your way." The Hawk raised his voice. "Aren't you, Mr. Dane?"

"Probably," came Dane's reply. "With the cavalry on the way, I might just find a place to sit and watch."

"You'll only be committing suicide if you try and stop us," Arkady said.

"I've survived too long to be scared off by talk like that. Hey, Cavallos, put the kettle on for me."

"You will indeed receive a proper welcome," Cavallos said.

Arkady turned off the radio in disgust.

Dane stepped through another hatch and looked down the long, narrow passage that would take him to the ship's bow. He started forward with an SR-2 Veresk in either hand, one pointed behind him and the other straight ahead. Nowhere to go in this passage, so any fight here could be his last. The walkway accommodated only one person, with the hull on one side and the inner wall of the interior storage bay on the other.

Dane advanced with confidence tempered by caution. Cavallos, his wife and remaining troops would be in the holding bay with Trent's laser. The fight could end there. For somebody.

The holding bay containing the M-113 with its mounted DEW also held stacked barrels and wooden crates, enough of a load to show customs if need be. For Cavallos it made a nice battleground. Plenty of cover. He had positioned himself and Roxana so they faced the connecting hatch between the bay they occupied and its immediate neighbor. That was one option Dane had to enter. The other hatch was across the hold and let out on the passageway. The other three troopers with Cavallos watched that hatch.

Minimal light lit the cargo hold and the low glow forced

Cavallos to engage his other senses. Hearing, mostly. He'd hear either hatch open before he saw it and judicious use of gunfire would take care of Steve Dane.

The only sounds penetrating the hull were the creaking of the steel and the crash of waves.

Cavallos's throat felt dry—a typical pre-combat condition. He looked around for Roxana but couldn't see her in the darkness.

The connecting hatch clicked and opened with a loud squeak that echoed through the hold. Cavallos and his wife fired into the hatch opening, two short bursts each.

Cavallos shouted, "Cover me!" and hopped from behind cover. He approached the open hatch with a flashlight, shining the light for two seconds. No Dane. He cursed.

Across the hold, the other hatch opened. Gunfire thundered.

Chapter Forty-Six

It wasn't much of a ruse, but any distraction that gave him any sort of edge, Dane certainly welcomed.

The bright lights in the passageway made stepping into the cargo hold like diving into an abyss, but Dane moved for cover as he fired both submachine guns. Return fire crackled, rounds tearing into crates and whining off walls. The ricochets continued well after the firing stopped.

Dane's eyes adjusted and he crawled forward on knees and elbows, bumping into a trooper also on the floor. Dane shot the man in the face.

A muzzle flashed to his left. Dane fired that way. The muzzle flash moved, and Dane fired to either side, a trooper screaming as he fell.

Dane dropped flat to reload.

How many more?

Movement to the right. A shuffling step, the outline of a man in the low light. Dane winged a shot that way, missed, the bullet bouncing off the wall to zing across the hold. The trooper, staying low, fired back, but Dane rolled away. He slammed into a steel barrel, jarring the other barrels stacked on top. He scrambled to his feet and ran as the top two fell over and landed with an echoing crash, exposing Dane. He fired a long burst at the trooper behind him, who fired back, the return fire splintering a nearby crate and sending slivers of wood into Dane's bare chest. He dropped behind the crate, fired over the top, missed again. The trooper moved right, tripped over the fallen barrels. Dane triggered both Veresks and hosed the area. The steel barrels took the hits with loud clangs, the cacophony of the shooting drowning out the trooper's scream.

Dane ceased fire, hunkered down and reloaded. Three down. Was that all? Which one had been Cavallos?

Dane remained still, the ringing in his ears making it hard to get a sense of whether or not he was alone. Then a radio squawked across the hold. Arkady's voice. Coast Guard choppers in sight. "Where is Dane? Where are *you*?"

Arkady's call continued with no answer.

Dane jumped up and ran to the M-113. He'd rode aboard many M-113s in the Marines but this one looked obviously different, with the 680c controls on the passenger side. He found the power switch, and the control panel sprang to life. A monitor displayed crosshairs lined up on the far wall of the hold. Dane used the joystick to reposition the dish, and heard small motors purring above the roof as the weapon responded to his input.

Three switches under a label reading "Fire Control" received Dane's attention next. He flipped each switch. A hum joined the motors, and the motors stopped once Dane had the weapon aimed at the floor a few feet ahead of the M-113. Something flashed on the monitor below the crosshairs, two words: "Stand By."

Gauges on the panel swung from green to yellow to red. The hum continued.

Dane caught movement outside the cabin and dived below the dash. Automatic weapons fire from two points smashed into the cabin, careening off the steel and punching cleanly through the Plexiglas. The DEW target monitor exploded, bits and pieces flying in all directions.

The two figures outside the M-113 moved closer, the light hitting them just right. Cavallos and Roxana. Dane stayed low and reached for the joystick. He clamped a finger on the trigger.

Nothing happened.

He still heard the hum. Had the gunfire damaged the weapon? He pulled the trigger again and again. Still no response.

Dane dropped from the cabin, firing over the hood. Cavallos and Roxana dived for cover. Dane ran for the hatch he'd entered from, rounds splitting the air around him. His feet caught on something, the body of a dead trooper, and he fell face-first onto the floor, the submachine guns flying from his grasp. He lay there, winded, feeling like a mule had kicked him in the gut.

Dane rolled onto his back, drawing the SIG P-226 9-millimeter. A figure with an obvious female shape ran his way. He fired twice. The woman yelped and hit the floor, unmoving.

"Roxana!"

Dane rose to crouch behind a crate. He looked over the top. Cavallos broke cover and ran in front of the M-113. He fired at Dane, who fired back, and then the floor exploded. Dane fell back, landing hard on his rear, as the DEW let off another silent pulse and a second explosion rocked the cargo hold.

Dane rose to hands and knees. A third pulse was coming, assuming the three times he'd pulled the trigger meant something. As he cleared the hatch and started down the passage, the third blast occurred. The ship shook and Dane lost his footing, slamming into the hull wall. He fell to his knees, the grating of the walkway tearing open his skin. He screamed, falling forward. The ship continued to rock, listing a little further to port than starboard. Getting up, Dane gripped the 9-millimeter pistol in his right hand and started to run. He had to neutralize Arkady before the Coast Guard landed.

Macedo and Storey, the Coast Guard pilots in the Ocean Sentry, still orbiting near the ship, reported the bow explosions. Flames flashed from one of the cargo areas. The choppers en route aimed for a middle-deck landing instead and made a circle around the ship to improve their approach.

Dane rose from a deck hatch near the superstructure, the wind slamming into him, cooling the sweat on his skin. The sun blinded him, and he squinted against the glare. He waved at the choppers and pointed at the deck. Not that the gesture didn't mean he wasn't a member of the ungodly, but perhaps any uncertainty would give him a moment to explain his presence.

The ship started to list deeper to the port side as Dane climbed the superstructure's outer ladder, passing through gaps in the exterior walkways on his way to the bridge. Smoke drifted his way, stinging his eyes. He coughed but kept climbing. The rotor blast from the two choppers blew the smoke away, and when the helicopters set down, side doors open, four men exited each. The raiders wore commando black with the usual tactical gear and weapons, and they ran toward the superstructure.

Dane cleared the last walkway and ran to the bridge

hatch. He wrenched it open and charged in with his pistol ready.

The sailors yelled, "Don't shoot!" and dropped to the floor, but Captain Sokolov drew a gun. Dane shot him in the head. As the captain's body dropped, Dane locked eyes on the Hawk. Defiance flashed in Arkady's eyes. He dived for Sokolov's pistol. Dane let him get his hands on it before he fired once more. The bullet caved in that hawkish nose before tearing out the back of the Russian's head, and Arkady fell on top of the captain.

Chapter Forty-Seven

The chief engineer shut off the engine and sealed the bow so the water flooding into the ship didn't go too far. The container vessel remained as still as the waves allowed, the front end submerged well above the waterline.

The strike team held Dane and the surviving crew members at gunpoint while they awaited an approaching cutter. The prisoners sat with their hands secured behind their backs. Dane made no effort to explain anything.

Once they were all aboard the cutter, a guardsman placed Dane in his own cell. The ship made for Texas. Dane remained under guard the whole time.

At the Coast Guard station on the Texas side of the gulf, they moved Dane to a holding cell, where he spotted a familiar face, the Frenchman who had pointed a gun at him in Florida until he admitted Number One and his pals into the hotel room. The Frenchman showed the on-site commander some papers. The commander made a few calls. Then a young guardsman let Dane out, and the commander placed Dane in the custody of the Frenchman. The Frenchman drove Dane away in a Ford sedan.

"You look like hell, *monsieur*," the Frenchman said.

Dane examined his chest and legs. Welts. Dried sweat. Dirt and grime. His knees ripped open, the dried blood a coagulated mess. He sure did look like hell. But he still lived, while he'd sent Arkady to a different kind of hell. Dane figured he'd come out ahead.

The Frenchman checked Dane into a local hospital for a checkup. Nina found him there while he was sitting on an examining table. She rushed into his arms and he squeezed her tight.

"What happened?" she said.

"All the baddies are dead, honey."

"McConn's here, too. He's a little woozy from surgery but he'll be okay."

The doctor entered the room and shooed her out.

Within twenty-four hours, Dane was out of the hospital and back in normal clothes, though not moving very fast and bandaged in several places. McConn, on crutches, joined him and Nina at the hotel.

Sitting up in bed, Dane called Trent.

"Are you okay?" said Trent.

"All is well. I'll spare you details for now."

"I know some."

"I'm afraid you'll have to rebuild your weapon."

"I don't need it anymore."

"Why not?"

"I had a visit from three friends of yours last night. Older gentlemen."

"Okay."

"They have put me in touch with some venture capital people who are very interested in how my company can improve laser-based medical devices. Apparently research my daughter has done has not gone unnoticed."

"The *deus ex machina* is clanking a little," Dane said, "so you might want to change the oil, but it seems to have worked for you."

Trent laughed. "You have my eternal gratitude."

"I'll pass that along and give our best to your daughter."

Dane hung up and told Nina and McConn. McConn, at the table with his bandaged leg propped up on the bed, saluted with a beer.

"Not a bad job," McConn said.

Nina sat beside Dane and snuggled close. Dane offered only a weak smile.

Colleen Trent heard a knock at the door and muted the television. Rising from the couch, she went to answer.

Her father stood there.

She said hello and let him in; he kissed her cheek and she moved to the kitchen offered coffee. He said he wasn't there to visit.

"Why are you here then?"

"I thought," he said, "we could go fishing."

Colleen Trent beamed.

Dane lay awake in bed that night with Nina snoring beside him. McConn had long before departed to his own room on another floor.

His cell phone lit up and vibrated. Dane took the phone into the bathroom. He leaned against the counter, wincing a little, and answered.

"Up a little late, aren't you, Mr. President?"

President Cross laughed. "I figured this would be the best time."

"Are you up to speed?"

"Yes and thank you."

"I assume the bodies and the survivors will be quietly returned to Moscow?"

"Arrangements in progress," Cross said. "You could have taken Arkady alive, you know."

"You know why I didn't, sir. The last thing we need is living proof of what happened and somebody to find out Putin himself ordered the theft. The survivors won't know anything more than what they were ordered to do. This way the major players are dead, it's covered up, and we can save a little face. In other words, we've avoided a war."

"You still put your country first, Steve."

"I put the balance of power first. We all know what Putin is doing, but there's no point in rushing into a fight right now."

"Have you spoken with our friends?"

"They have my number, sir."

"I'll light those candles like you asked."

"We appreciate it."

"What are your plans now?"

"Wait for that other call, first. I think we'll be in the US for a while."

"Call me when you get to Washington."

"I will. Good night, sir."

Dane returned to the bed and finally dozed off. His cell did not ring again.

Dane and Nina quietly ate breakfast the next morning, the window open, morning sounds drifting in. Chirping birds, car engines; quiet and tranquil. Just what the doctor ordered after the events of the previous day. Then a knock on the door. Dane froze with a sausage halfway to his mouth. Nina didn't pause. "I'm not getting up," she said.

Dane answered and the Frenchman entered with The Trust behind him.

"You have a habit of interrupting my meals," Dane said as the three old men found seats.

"We won't be here long," said Number One, sitting on the edge of the bed. He said to Nina, "So you're the one I talked to."

"We didn't wait very long for help," she said. "I'm impressed."

"Friends in high places come in handy, don't they, Mr. Dane?"

"Sure," Dane said. "I appreciate you breaking me out of the Coast Guard."

"It was nothing that dramatic. We told the commander you couldn't be there, since you didn't really exist."

"Funny how that works."

"Any thoughts on our original discussion?"

"I will honor the deal. One job for you in exchange for what you promised me. And if things go well, maybe a job now and then, too."

"The job will come eventually," said Number One. "Here is our end of the deal." The old man took a folded piece of paper from his shirt pocket. Dane took it from the offered hand.

He unfolded it.

"A man's name?"

"You remember him, of course."

"Yes."

"That's where you start."

Dane blinked a few times. There was a lot he could have said, but actual words failed him. He folded the paper and ran his finger along the edge.

"Once you arrive," Number one said, "you'll know

what to do."

Dane nodded and let out a breath.

"It's time to answer questions I've been asking for a long time," he said.

Number One turned to Nina. "And what about you, Miss Talikova?"

"What about me?" she said.

"Once we are done with Mr. Dane's enterprise, we would be happy to devote our resources to your cause."

"I wasn't aware I had one."

A half smile crossed Number One's face. "We know what happened in Moscow, Miss Talikova. You might say the two of you are on a collision course with what made you."

Nina folded her arms. If looks could kill, the frown she gave Number One would have put him in the morgue.

The half-smile faded from the old man's face.

"Of course. But you are not ready. We understand."

"I'd like it if you left," she said.

Dane, sitting still, made no move to argue with her.

Number One said, "Be seeing you," and departed with his crew. They quietly shut the door behind them.

Dane felt Nina's eyes on him but remained still.

"I need a drink," Nina said.

She left the table and retrieved a bottle of Russian Standard from the dresser. Dane didn't stop her.

A collision course with what made them. Dane played with the words in his head. He couldn't escape the past. He couldn't run forever. Those who tried had to pay a price. Was he paying that price? Had the mental torture, the unknown what-ifs of his life, finally taken their toll, with the guiding hand of the universe now forcing him into action?

He unfolded the piece of paper and looked at the name again. *Burn the paper*, he thought. *Pretend it doesn't exist. Pretend you don't know.*

But what toll would come due if he did?

He watched Nina pop open the vodka and pour a generous portion into her orange juice. She took a long drink. When she set her glass down, their eyes met.

Dane wasn't sure what she saw in his eyes, but what he saw in her eyes was crystal clear.

Fear.

A Look At: Live To Kill: A Steve Dane Thriller

Steve Dane faces a day of reckoning long coming when he learns the truth about his father.

But the truth is a bitter pill when he discovers his father's death ties to rogue agents within US intelligence who use Agency assets to further their own agenda. With battle lines drawn, Steve Dane and Nina Talikova do what they do best: attack! From the shores of Maryland to the blistering heat of a South American jungle, Dane and Nina destroy each tentacle of the enemy before finally coming face to face with the top dog himself, and a final, crippling betrayal.

Will Dane be able to do what is required?

AVAILABLE AUGUST 2021

About the Author

A twenty-five year veteran of radio and television broadcasting, Brian Drake has spent his career in San Francisco where he's filled writing, producing, and reporting duties with stations such as KPIX-TV, KCBS, KQED, among many others. Currently carrying out sports and traffic reporting duties for Bloomberg 960, Brian Drake spends time between reports and carefully guarded morning and evening hours cranking out action/adventure tales. He lives in California with his wife and two cats, and when he's not writing he is usually blasting along the back roads in his Corvette with his wife telling him not to drive so fast, but the engine is so loud he usually can't hear her.